Berji Kristin

Tales from the Garbage Hills

To Ertuğrul

Berji Kristin

Tales from the Garbage Hills

a novel by

Latife Tekin

Preface by John Berger
Introduction by Saliha Paker
Translated from the Turkish by
Ruth Christie and Saliha Paker

Marion Boyars
London · New York

Reprinted in Great Britain and the United States in 2015 by
MARION BOYARS PUBLISHERS LTD
26 Parke Road, London SW13 9NG

www.marionboyars.co.uk

First published in hard cover in Great Britain and the United States in 1993
by Marion Boyars Publishers, London

Originally published in Turkey as *Berci Kristin Cöp Masallari* in 1984
by Metis Yayinlari, Istanbul

Reprinted in 1996, 2004, 2015
10 9 8 7 6 5 4 3 2

A CIP catalogue record for this book is available from the British Library.
A CIP catalog record for this book is available from the Library of Congress.

ISBN 978-0-7145-3011-6

Printed in Great Britain by the CPI Group.

Rumour
Preface by John Berger

I have never read another book like this one. And perhaps you haven't either. True originality is unusually difficult to define because it gives the impression of existing for the first time and this — fortunately — precludes generalizations. Within an original work you lose your way. If you stay with it, you are captured, you are forced to reside there, and the experience becomes unforgettable. If you don't like losing your way, you shut the book, you mutter Nonsense! and it remains closed to you, probably for ever.

It was several years ago I first lost my way in Latife Tekin's book. I had already lost my way many times in Istanbul, the city she writes about. I was visiting people in the shanty-towns. I was often on the Bosphorus ferry plying between Asia and Europe. My feet got dusty with exactly the dust of the earth she describes. And suddenly what I was watching, what I was brushing shoulders with, what I was turning my back on, what I would never see, what I was deaf to, was given a voice in her book. A book in which I again lost myself, but this time in the labyrinth of her understanding.

Several years later, through mutual Turkish friends, we met, Latife and I. And during an entire evening we kept on laughing. Laughing, I think, at the inexplicable. For example, we'd have laughed a lot — if we'd known about it then — at the idea of my writing a preface to her book!

We were laughing partly because, without a proper common language between us, laughter was the best alternative to silence. (For different reasons, this is often the case in this book.) But also we were laughing at everything that can never be said anywhere. Two writers at the end of their tether, laughing about it. Such laughter is very Mediterranean. It begins where lucidity and sunlight say the same thing.

Of course Latife Tekin didn't set out to be original. If the thought ever crossed her mind, it would have been before she was thirteen. Artists who retain such an ambition are ones who never grow up. The originality of Tekin's mature book is the direct consequence of its story. Before her, no shanty-town had entered literature — had entered written narrative — as an entity in itself. If shanty-towns were there, they were there as décor or as social problems. In Tekin's *Tales From The Garbage Hills* a shanty-town community becomes the centre of the world, holding the stage and addressing the sky.

She has written down what before had never been written down. Other books by other writers will follow — perhaps have already followed — but their and our debt to her is enormous. It isn't that she showed the way. We all lose our way and there are a hundred ways. But she showed that it was possible, possible for any reader anywhere in the world, to at last imagine the centre of the world as a shanty-town! If you want to do that, read this book.

It's about language. Not because Latife is a post-modernist or a structuralist, but because she is familiar with the lives lived on the garbage hills. She knows deeply how nick-names, stories, rumours, jingles, gossip, jokes, repartees constitute a kind of home, even the most solid home, when everything else is temporary, makeshift, illegal, shifting and without a single guarantee. Wind, dust, wind. Yet the Tales save from oblivion more effectively than the roofs give shelter. Everything is polluted on the hills except the legendary names people earn with their lives, and the laughter provoked by those names. On the garbage hills laughter takes the arm of heartbreak. And death is venomous and everywhere.

The story-teller of the Tales is rumour. As a means of expression rumour is not much approved of in places where certitudes rule. Law courts. Ministries. The offices of managing directors. Colleges. Rumour is worse than myth for it is uncontrollable. The only big institution where rumour is rife is the Stock Exchange. The stock brokers deal with (and create) events in a nexus which is volatile, unpredictable, often inexplicable, risky and packed (over-populated with money). Rumour is a mass reaction to trying to follow, anticipate and hold together events which are always on the brink of chaos. This is why — astonishingly — Wall Street and the garbage hills have one thing in common. The noise of rumour.

Otherwise of course they are the opposite poles of this planet, one occupied by winners, the other by losers: one set of rumours signalling the best way to make money, and the other set of rumours whispering about the latest crazy slender hope of survival. The first on the verge of mental breakdown — as the pharmaceutical record shows. The second on the verge of fairy story – so long as one remembers that fairy stories, when first told, were as cruel as life.

Rumour is born of the irrepressible force of a community's imagination deprived of shelter or any guarantees. And Latife Tekin has found here the voice of rumour. I don't know how she found that shanty voice. But it came to her like genius. There are comparable pages by Joyce where he found the male voice of drunken rumour. Tekin's rumour is feminine and sober. Never maudlin. Never shocked. Never rhetorical. Never flinching. As if rumour were an angel with a sword.

She walks blindfolded through wherever people gather on the hills — the car battery factory, the brickworks, the linen factory, Nato Avenue, the detergent factory, the hen houses, the grocery stores, the trade union meetings, the mosques, the cardboard homes, the brothels. Blindfolded and dry-eyed, she hears and therefore sees all.

Why say angel? She brings a promise that nobody can not believe in and yet nobody thinks true. The promise is that again and again, from the garbage, the scattered feathers, the ashes and the broken bodies, something new and beautiful may be born. Perhaps rumour here is a demon, not an angel — for she cannot stop raising hopes which do not last. But wherever I fell in this world, I would pray for her, angel or demon, to come and I would listen to her and she would revive me as she revives so many . . .

Introduction
by Saliha Paker

When Latife Tekin's first book, *Dear Cheeky Death
(Sevgili Arsız Ölüm)* came out in 1983, breaking through the
cloud of silence after the military intervention of 1980, it
was hailed as 'magic'. This term implied a degree of
astonishment on the part of the critical establishment: some
affinity with Marquezian fiction, yes, but also something
unique in the way a Turkish writer was exploiting fantasy
which was not a means of escapism but of reconstructing an
individual experience that was authentic and indigenous.
The following introduction, written by Tekin herself for the
first edition of her book, gives an insight into her background and way of writing:

'I was born in 1957 in the village of Karacafenk, near the
town of Bünyan in the province of Kayseri. I started school
as soon as I learned to walk. The school was the men's
living room in our house. I learned to read and write as I

played with the jinn under the divans. Jinn and fairies used to live under the divans in Karacefenk. I spent my childhood among them, secretly joining their community. I went to see their homes, their weddings, and learned their language, their day games and night games. My father used to work in Istanbul. I forget now who told me that my mother was a strange woman with a broken heart. She was literate, sewed, gave injections, and knew Kurdish and Arabic. She used to enquire from the gypsies that came to the village about places and people unknown to me. Her searchings for her past were the first pains that touched my childhood. My father used to come back from Istanbul with sacks full of money and gathered the villagers. Our house was full of strange gadgets, magic metals. I had no idea of their use. . .

'In 1966 I came to live in Istanbul. It felt like a sharp pain that split up my childhood. Unfulfilled dreams tore apart the people that I grew up with. My father quickly became working class, then gradually fell into unemployment. Three brothers worked on construction sites. I finished high school, slipping away like a trembling shadow from seven brothers and sisters. I paid the price of moving away from fear and loneliness to go to school: subjected to a thousand denials and pressures, I was incredibly shaken. I fought hard to keep up with the city and was badly bruised. During my struggles I fell apart from those that I grew up with. But I resisted in order not to lose my own values, my language, and the constant and passionate love that those people bore me. This book is my reward from the people I grew up with for my resistance. . .'

Dear Cheeky Death was based on Tekin's childhood and adolescent experiences of the village and of the outskirts of the metropolis, and it was unlike anything that had previously been written in the genre of rural or urban fiction. The 'Village Novel' had been established as a major genre in Turkish fiction since the 1950s in the predominant mode of social/ist realism, focusing on the problems and dynamics of rural society from the 'enlightened' point of view of the educated writer of peasant origin with a mission. The rural fiction of Yaşar Kemal transcended this genre in its use of myth and in epic scope and style. The urban novel, on the other hand, bore the stamp of the 'intellectual' left-wing author, chiefly concerned with the tensions brought about by social change, political conflict, and by a republican ideology based on westernization. The novel itself was an adopted genre, introduced from Western literature in the second half of the 19th century when the Ottoman Empire came under political and economic pressures, and social and cultural influences from Europe. It was used initially as a vehicle for a critical attitude towards family and society, differences between Eastern and Western values and ways of life, and represented a reaction to the fantasy and escapism of the Eastern romance. An acute sense of realism, however, did not emerge till the early years of the new, proud but poverty stricken republic founded (1923) on the remains of the Empire that fell at the end of the first World War. By the 1950s, social realism had become the formative mode determining the conventions of the modern Turkish novel, regardless of the urban/rural distinction. Society was the sacred area of concern in the novel while the inner world of the individual found its best expression in the short story. Since the 1960s, however, both the novel and the short story have gained a rich diversity in subject matter, scope and style while still holding on to the realistic tradition. This is largely due to the proliferation in fiction by women who have proved to be less fearful of exploring new ground. While some boldly imaginative women writers in the 1960s came under critical pressure, either stopped writing for a long time or changed their course and fell more in line with mainstream fiction, others more confident in the 1970s went their own way. Barriers against introspection, fantasy and sexuality were broken down.

Even in this broader context, however, Latife Tekin stood as a challenge to the mainstream fiction of the 1980s by rejecting 'realism' in favour of a highly metaphorical perception of reality in which fantasy is an essential element. In conjunction with fresh narrative forms, Tekin developed a figurative style which is vigorous and innovative. She has often expressed the desire to forge 'a language of the deprived', one that gives expression not only to their way of life but also to their outlook on life, perception of reality, sense of humour and dreams. In this respect *Berji Kristin*, her second book (1984), can be considered a breakthrough in modern Turkish fiction.

In *Berji Kristin: Tales from the Garbage Hills*, the squatter settlements built on rubbish tips may appear bizarre or unreal to some readers, but in fact refer to a 'real' phenomenon in the Istanbul of the 1960s. In the experience of millions who, since the 1960s, have been flowing into the big cities to make a living, squatterland was an extension of the village. But as seen in *Berji Kristin* life there, unlike in the village, had different dynamics and was subject to sharply dramatic as well as gradual changes. Makeshift dwellings could be set up overnight ('*gecekondu*', the Turkish word for squatter hut, means 'set up/perched overnight') but razed to the ground the next day. Even in the 1990s it is not uncommon to have police raids on squatter huts built on land unlawfully possessed. Such news, accompanied by photographs conveying the drama especially of women and children torn away from their homes, still make the headlines. While struggles continue, especially in pockets or frontiers, the primitive dwellings of thirty years ago have been transformed into two or three storey buildings, roads have been built, public transport has been provided by local authorities. But 'Rubbish Road' has remained the name of a bus stop on the main road from the Bosphorus to the city, the mosque with the tin minaret was still standing in 1988, and those who witnessed the survival of the baby whose cradle landed on a treetop, have themselves survived to pass on their 'tales' to their sons and daughters. Tekin's narrative, akin to the oral tradition of the '*masal*' (fairy/folk tale) is based on the testimony of the older generation of squatters who witnessed the genesis of a subculture of enormous social significance despite its marginal situation. Assuming the position of a detached but devoted narrator rather than a patronizing intellectual onlooker, Tekin has reconstructed the dreams and realities of squatterland in specific detail and with a uniquely metaphoric use of the language, without overlooking the humorous attitudes, ironic perception and emotional vitality of the community amid the filth and poverty of its living conditions. The squatter settlement, which had so far existed in Turkish fiction as the periphery whose inhabitants were taken into account in terms of the social class they represented, became in *Berji Kristin* a world of its own.

This is essentially a man's world, but women appear in it as strangely powerful figures, despite their subordination. Their world in Tekin's fiction maintains a distinctive interaction with its male counterpart and womanhood is conceived as a secret society resisting and, at times, subverting oppressive forces. However, like the majority of

Turkish women writers, Tekin makes no claim to feminism in the Western sense, which is regarded as a separating and restricting factor for a fiction writer. What lies behind this stance are the specific conditions created by a secularist ideology of a republican state (which tends to shun any form of separation or segregation), the desire for total social involvement, and the need to address a wide readership. It is interesting, for instance, that in *Berji Kristin* the rise and decline of the community on the garbage hills is symbolized by the female attributions in the title: 'Berji' for innocence, and 'Kristin' for prostitution.

The rich variations in Latife Tekin's language, which give expression to a powerfully creative inner voice, will inevitably be recognized as having sparked off the imagination of a whole new generation of writers, regardless of gender. Following the trends in the West, the impressive works of Orhan Pamuk, for instance, appear as a subtle challenge to the conventional novel from within the mainstream, but the making of the modern Turkish novel has also to account for the consistently unpredictable originality of such writers as Latife Tekin.

One winter night, on a hill where the huge refuse bins came daily and dumped the city's waste, eight shelters were set up by lantern-light near the garbage heaps. In the morning the first snow of the year fell, and the earliest scavengers saw these eight huts pieced together from materials bought on credit — sheets of pitchpaper, wood from building sites, and breezeblocks brought from the brickyards by horse and cart. Not even stopping to drop the sacks and baskets from their backs, they all ran to the huts and began a lively exchange with the squatters who were keeping watch. A harsh and powerful wind kept cutting short their words and at one point almost swept the huts away. The scavengers pointed out that the ramshackle walls and makeshift roofs would never stand up to the wind, so the squatters decided to rope down the roofs and nail supports to the walls.

When the garbage trucks had come and gone, the simit-sellers on the way to the garbage heard that eight huts had been built on the slopes and spread the news through the neighbouring warehouses, workshops and coffee houses. By noon people had begun to descend on the hillside like snow. Janitors, pedlars and simit-sellers all arrived with pickaxes, closely followed by people who had left their villages to move in with their families in the city, and by others roaming the hills behind the city in the hope of building a hut. Men and women, young and old, spread in all directions. Kneeling and rising they measured with feet and outstretched arms. Then with their spades they scratched crooked plans in the earth. By evening Rubbish Road had become a road of bricks and blocks and pitchpaper. That night in snowfall and lantern-light a hundred more huts were erected in the snow.

Next morning, by the garbage heaps — downhill from the factories which manufactured lightbulbs and chemicals, and facing the china factory — a complete neighbourhood was fathered by mud and chemical waste, with roofs of plastic basins, doors from old rugs, oilcloth windows and walls of wet breezeblocks.

Throughout the day bits and pieces arrived to furnish the houses, and the remaining women and children, with sacks on their backs and babies in arms, entered their homes. Mattresses were unrolled and kilim-rugs spread on the earthen floors. The damp walls were hung with faded pictures and brushes with their blue bead good-luck charms, cradles were slung from the roofs and a chimney pipe was knocked through the sidewall of every hut.

The factory workers gathered at the windows to watch, laughing at the belongings arriving in horse-drawn carts and the people chasing up and down. All day long there were whistles, catcalls, jeers. In the evening a weariness settled on the huts and the inhabitants dozed off under the wet walls, and the roofs creaked in the wind. By the time the factory nightshift had left, the founders of the community were fast asleep. The factory machinery had stopped; lights were out. The hill was engulfed in pitch darkness, but in the small hours a wind sneaked up, loosened the rooftops, and carried them away. And the babies too, asleep in the roof-cradles, flew off along with the roofs.

The hut people woke with snow falling on their lashes and faces still warm from deep sleep. They thought at first they were having a wonderful dream; the sky had turned to snow and filled their huts. Then their cries rent the night. Men and women, old and young, rushed out in their underwear; lanterns were lit; everyone turned out to search for roofs and babies. Keening and lamenting, the women tied magic knots in their handkerchiefs and headscarves to arrest the passage of the wind, praying it would carry the babies no further.

One roof was found in the garden of the lightbulb factory, come to rest and stuck between two mulberry trees. The baby from the roof-cradle was hoarse from crying and its eyes were enormous with fear. The other roofs were lined up side by side on the level ground around the china factory and the babies were out of their cradles, crawling about in the snow and playing with broken shards. In the wind the clatter mingled with their shrill little cries.

Fervently the women hugged their ice-cold babies and sheltered in a coal shed a little way off. The men dragged the roofs back, one or two at a time and, lifting them over the walls, tethered them with stout ropes and secured them with battens to prevent them flying off again. They wound the ropes round the legs of the long seats which lined their walls, and whenever the wind blew hard they hung on tight and pulled on the ropes and battens.

While they were securing the roofs and praying they would not fly off, all the birds of the city flocked together to the Wood-and-Plastic Neighbourhood. They circled round the huts and mocked the roofs that wished to sprout the wings of a bird:

> *Wee wee rooftops,*
> *Won't you wing with me?*
> *Drop the babies' cradles*
> *And fly away free.*
> *Fling us out a wee one,*
> *Wee, wee, wee!*

For days the birds circled and swooped over the huts, their wheeling and screeching betraying the site. And while they flew and mocked '*wee wee wee*', the demolition men arrived on the hill.

'Don't bunch together: we'll be sitting ducks and they'll raze our homes to the ground.'

The women dropped their babies and picked up hatchets, the men held shovel handles at the ready and took up positions in front of the huts. A lame woman struck the first blow at a wrecker kicking down the wall of one of the huts. He lay bleeding on the ground, then over and over he rolled down and down to the stream. The hut people hurled themselves in a body at the wreckers, and the fluttering birds flew up to the clouds. The wreckers dropped their pickaxes and fled down to the stream.

That night huge trucks arrived and a jeep followed by five trucks made its way between the huts. Headlamps were switched on, and the hut people were summoned to the headlights at gunpoint.

'Don't bunch together, if they surround us we're finished!'

The fight lasted nearly an hour but the hut people were finally surrounded and trapped in the light of the headlamps. Belongings vanished under the wreckage of their homes and in the early morning light all the people were crammed into trucks and driven away.

When the trucks had gone the birds who came to play among the roofs glided from the sky, and feathers bedewed with tears fluttered down on the ravaged huts. Then they swooped away.

In the afternoon all those who had been removed in the trucks came back to the hill of demolished huts. They wandered sadly about amongst their broken, scattered belongings which the scavengers and the wind had picked to bits, tossed aside and blown in all directions. At first they wept tears of rage, then threw themselves angrily into action. They rapidly reassembled the fragments of wood, cobbled the torn kilims and nailed together bits of tin while the children collected stones, unbroken breezeblocks and bricks and piled them up. That night they erected new huts half the size of those demolished. On the roofs they spread spoils from the garbage heap, bits of plastic, tattered cotton rugs and kilims and, dragging fragments of broken crockery up from the flat ground below the china factory, they used them as tiles. They retired to their new homes after midnight, weary and disheartened and drifted into sleep listening to the shards singing in the wind.

But the fragments on the roof fell off one by one, the kilims and bits of plastic blew away and were scattered far and wide. Water seeped between the breezeblocks and formed pools in the middle of the huts. A flurry of snow fell through the gaping roofs onto the cradles, but no one, woke till the babies began to cry. So the women got up at last and

lit the broken lamps. They dug a ditch in each hut to channel off the dammed-up water, brushed the snow from the mattresses and covered the roofs with rugs and rags.

Towards morning, unable to resist the wind any longer, one of the huts collapsed. The baby who had flown off with the roof into the factory garden was killed, trapped between fragments of stone and wood. In the morning they wrapped the child in an old quilt. Three men carried the bundle to a distant graveyard and leapt stealthily over the cemetery wall, but the baby gently abandoned the quilt and took wing. The mother tore her hair and ripped open her bodice. Filling her skirt with stones, she climbed to the hilltop where she cursed the wind and pelted it with stones till they had to drag her away. And from that day the hill was known as Wind-Curse Point.

In the early hours of the morning the children would gather on Wind-Curse Point and look out for the wreckers. One morning they flew down from the hill like birds and announced that a gang of men carrying gleaming pickaxes were heading straight for the huts. Before anyone could draw breath the gleaming pickaxes had attacked the hut walls. The hut people hurled themselves at the wreckers but were stopped by the trucks and, in a single moment, earth and huts became one. The wreckers shouldered their pickaxes and left, the trucks withdrew. The chilly light of day pierced the rubble and, as the roar of the engines faded, they all heard a thin, tremulous cry.

Sırma stood trembling before the ruins, embracing a complete, undamaged brick. As the other children gathered stones and bits of tin all over the hill, her trembling increased. Then she began to struggle and kick. She put down the brick and lay on it, tearing out handfuls of hair and throwing them to the wind. The women made a circle round her and tied her hands together. Holding her by her rough and matted hair, they shook her, scooped water on her face and stuffed a rag in her mouth to stop her teeth locking together. Exhausted with struggling, she fell quietly on the ground, her hands tied, and her eyes enormous. The women lit a fire and until morning she watched the people reassemble the huts by the dim light. In the morning Sırma's mother dragged her to their own rebuilt hut, covered her up and untied her hands.

In the morning the wreckers came back. The hut people, bent double and collapsed with exhaustion, started up at the sound of approaching bulldozers. Blinking with fear, they dragged themselves from their huts and flung out mattresses and kilims and whatever was left. The bulldozers rolled methodically backwards and forwards over the huts, reducing the fragments of china and bricks to a fine dust, splintering the wood into neat fragments, and hurling aside the crumpled pieces of tin.

The bulldozers went roaring off as they had come, and the trucks withdrew. The workers watching from the factory windows went back to their machines without a word. As Sırma stood by the wreckage, she was seized with grief again and kicking up the brick dust behind the bulldozers, she plucked and tore her hair and dress and threw herself screaming on the ground. They tied her hands again and summoned the oldest member of the community, Güllü Baba, to recite the prayers which would heal her. He came feeling his way with his stick and squatting beside Sırma, he sought and found her twitching body. He turned his face towards the little girl shaking under his touch. Then he leant on his stick, murmured a long incantation and blew on her the breath of healing. As her tremors stilled under his touch, his heart suddenly swelled and, like Sırma, he too was seized by grief. When she shook and stretched her bound hands, he also shook. Then she saw tears pouring from Güllü Baba's shrunken eyes, and she quietened and stopped shaking. Güllü Baba wiped his eyes and was quiet too. He bent down and held her bound hands and breathed on her mud-streaked face, saying 'Don't cry, little dove, they'll free your hands; go and gather lots of tin.' They untied her hands, and she made her way quietly through the surrounding crowd and began to collect the tin.

Behind her the people dispersed on the hill. In a moment the old plaster moulds and debris from the china factory turned into walls again. The men picked quarrels with the scavengers who ran away down to the stream. Plastic bags and baskets provided roofs for the huts; homes were built part rubble, part moulds, part shards. In the morning the wreckers kicked them to the ground. By night the hut people had erected mounds from all kinds of materials they had salvaged during the day from the garbage: metal, stone, wood. But in the morning the wreckers returned and razed them all to the ground again.

The destruction went on for exactly thirty-seven endless days, and after each raid the huts became a little smaller and gradually lost all resemblance to houses. The hut people seemed no longer human, smeared with dust, mud, garbage, their clothes in rags. Three babies died, weary of cold and destruction, and took wing to heaven before the very eyes of the wreckers. One old woman who had wounded one of the wreckers with a hatchet was marched off between two policemen and removed from the hill. The survivors were nearly dead from picking over the garbage and collecting pieces of tin.

Towards the end, not a single tree was left upright on the hill, and the garbage was reduced to shreds. Rusty tins, heads of light bulbs, china, cardboard boxes scavenged from the refuse, bottles, bits of plastic, and anything they could lay hands on, were all put to use in rebuilding the huts.

One morning they beat up a man who arrived in a snow-white car, introducing himself as Garbage Owner. They beat him up, and bits of flock from the torn mattresses stuck to the dried blood from his nose and mouth. There was nothing left now, neither mattress nor blankets, or shards of any use for building. The huts had become smaller and smaller; they were like dwarfs' houses, and those too were swept away by the wind.

Bitterly the hut people watched their homes vanish with the wind. That night they took refuge in one of the buildings under construction at the start of Rubbish Road. The women and children withdrew to a corner, and the men sat round Güllü Baba. Sadly he leant his head on his hand and pondered for a long, long time. Then he rested his cheek on his walking stick and muttered. He advised them to squat in the building until the wreckers had forgotten the whereabouts of the hill where they had built their huts.

'We'll lay claim to the garbage and set up homes,' he said.

Till late into the night they spoke of how they would collect bottles, bits of iron and plastic and sell them. As they talked, they saw gold and jewels in the garbage, then they closed their eyes dazzled with the glitter of precious stones and sank into sleep.

Wide awake, Sırma gazed into the dark and retraced a long train journey. She sat waiting with her mother under a stone bridge thinking all the passers-by looked like her elder brother. Gazing only at her brother's face, she saw neither the houses lining the wide streets nor the sea, and so she was utterly bewildered when they entered a house in the city far smaller than their home. She was embarrassed and all that day avoided her father.

That night Sırma's thoughts were full of the days when she had lived in her uncle's house, but with the first light of morning her thoughts evaporated and she quietly slipped away from her mother's arms and ran to the hill where their hut had stood. There she wandered about collecting broken glass, tiny stones, buttons, bottletops. Then she took a breath and sat down at the spot where she had torn her hair and out of the broken bits of glass, the old nylon comb with two teeth, the buttons and the bottletops, she made a tiny hut.

Later in the morning when the wreckers returned they saw a little girl on the hill playing house where the huts had been. They circled around her, then departed, and from that day on they never came back.

After giving the wreckers three days the hut people gathered at the garbage heap. They picked out a broken, splintered chunk of wood and with a piece of coal scrawled on it the letters 'Battle Hill'. Then they carried it down and hung it on the wall of a workshop at the top of Rubbish Road. A month later this wooden nameplate was removed by two official-looking men and replaced by a blue metal plaque inscribed FLOWER HILL.

After the renaming, people heard the demolition had stopped and came to the Hill in their hundreds, deceived by the charm of its name. Deep holes were dug in Rubbish Road to stop them, and sand and gravel were brought up in huge trucks and dumped. But the people who swarmed to the hill grabbed their shovels, filled in the holes with the sand and gravel and continued up the road. In one night by lantern-light, a hundred more huts were erected on Flower Hill and next morning all adjacent vacant lots were shared out and the allotments marked off with small stones and wire. The owners arrived in ones and twos, laden with belongings from their villages. They set up their huts and took possession.

Before the flowers opened on Flower Hill, three separate communities had sprung up from the huts — some of which stood face to face and others sulkily back to back. The children gave names to all three. They called them Factory Foot, Garbage Pit, and Rivermouth.

When Flower Hill broke into blossom, the first thing to be erected by daylight was a mosque with a minaret made of tin plate, but the very day the mosque went up the night wind tore it apart and blew it away. The rumour spread that if anyone found the minaret and brought it back, everything they touched would turn to gold, and many went without sleep to search hilltop and valley. But in spite of all the searching the minaret was never found. The discussion over the lost minaret lasted for days until finally a decision was reached to build a new one, and as a result of these discussions one more commandment was added to the Five Pillars of Islam, 'Thou shalt hold down the minaret at night.' It was decreed that children, the handicapped, nursing mothers and pregnant women would be excused from holding the minaret, and it would be counted a sin if they did.

One morning a stone with an inscription was uncovered behind the mosque on Factory Foot. Word spread through the huts that a saint lay under the stone, and it was considered an offence to urinate or spit on the spot or pass by without saying a prayer. The whole community went to the stone and prayed for water. Metal bowls and little tins were filled with water and lined up round the stone to show the saint what water was. They explained the difficulties of carrying water from wells on top of far-away hills in tins dangling from both ends of a yoke slung across their backs. Buttons were undone and backs bared, and everyone in turn showed the stone the calluses on their necks and backs. From then on they carried water to the stone and bared their backs with prayers and invocations. But not one drop of water could be had from 'Water Father' and in time people forgot they had ever prayed to him for water. Instead, childless women and those with wishes to be fulfilled took him whatever they could spare from the little water in their cans — until there were so many bowls and tins at Factory Foot that they blocked the way.

One of the chemical factories was built over Water Father who lay right under the warehouse for raw materials, so when the warehouse workers began to die of poison, Flower Hill believed they had incurred Water Father's anger.

In early summer, showers of pure white from this factory began to pour over Flower Hill. At first they thought it was snow and were amazed. Then an intolerable stench reached the huts and within three days this factory snow had withered the first blooms on Flower Hill and wilted the branches of trees. Hens curled up with drooping necks and died, and people were unable to hold their heads upright.

In the middle of playing, children turned dark purple as if drugged and fell into a deep sleep. One of the sleeping children never woke up.

For days the factory which rained snow was pelted with stones. Its garden wall was torn down, gates were smashed and windows broken. There were rumours that the factory owner was going to bring down the huts and clear the neighbourhood. Flower Hill exploded with anger. Women marched on the factory with clubs, and when they entered and failed to find the owner they knocked the workers to the ground and beat them up. For days the men kept watch on the road for a glimpse of the owner but it was a never-ending vigil. Over the huts the factory snow grew to six inches deep. One noon when Flower Hill was only half conscious from the foul stink, a gift of yoghurt in white bowls arrived for everybody from the owner, followed by a man in white who went round the huts one by one examining the people. They gave up cursing the owner and everyone raised their hands in prayer to him. Once rewarded with their prayers, he flooded the neighbourhood with the hot bluish water in which the factory serum and medicine bottles were washed. That was a truly festive day for Flower Hill. They diverted the first jet of hot water and cemented round the channel where it flowed. A fountain was built there and for three whole days clothes, kilims, scraps of wool, pots and pans were washed in the hot water, and the children bathed. Only Flower Hill had the good fortune to wash in blue hot water under snow on a summer's day. The men dragged an old truck chassis a long distance to the fountainhead and from then on married couples on the Hill took it in turns to get inside this chassis at night after intercourse and wash themselves in hot water. The enervating snow still fell, and in the light of the moon the blue water gleamed and splashed.

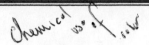

Before long, odd changes began to appear in those who washed in this water. The skin of some began to peel while the faces of others turned purple. Bright blue spots came out on the children's bodies and the hair of two women went white. The clothes took on a blue colour which came to be known on Flower Hill as 'Squatter's Blue'.

Squatter's Blue got into everything on Flower Hill. Lime for whitewashing the huts was mixed with the water and the huts, dyed blue, all looked alike and confused people. Then everyone put an individual mark on his hut; one inlaid the walls with coloured stones; another planted a tree in his garden; and another stuck a post in front of the hut and tied a rag to it. People were just becoming acquainted, so when they did not remember each other's names, they were called after their signs, like 'Waving Rag' and 'Inlaid Stone'. Some of the names were dropped altogether and forgotten and replaced by signs.

Ever since the first homes went up on Flower Hill, the women had organized nightly lantern groups. Lavatory pits had not yet been dug so they assembled and went off down to the stream together, initiating an entirely new custom as they went up and down. It was not done for women to go down to the stream in daytime and, if they saw a man bounding downhill, they giggled and shut their eyes. But when it was quite dark they quietly slipped out of their homes and tapped on each other's windows. Every night there was a long procession as the women emerged holding their lamps and skipped quietly down to the stream.

These were the earliest customs established on Flower Hill. In time other customs were added to do with unemployment, wind and garbage. Some took root and remained, others vanished.

At one baby's birth an argument over different customs and beliefs ended in a violent quarrel. Some women said that the baby girl arrived with Mother Fadime's veil, a lucky omen, and they maintained that the Bird of Luck would perch on the head of anyone who took the veil and hid it in their bosom for three days. They advised the recital of the Mevlut. Another said that a woman who put the veil under her pillow for three days and slept on it would lengthen her days. Yet another declared that if any woman held the veil in her hand or in her bosom she would never in her life be hit by a bullet. The baby's veil rose in value and got stolen, and immediately the child sickened. An old woman summoned to pray for the child said that unless the veil was found and put on its chest, the child would die in three days. In desperation Flower Hill chased after the veil to save the baby's life, but meantime the baby died. The mother rose from her childbed and stoned the huts: she rushed on every woman she saw. Some ran inside and closed their doors, others threw stones that cut her head. When the men interfered, a fierce fight suddenly broke out involving the three communities. The dispute jumped from adults to children and for a time no one could go out alone on Flower Hill.

Meanwhile refuse was dumped continuously on the Hill, and with the milder weather the seagulls forsook the garbage. Amidst their shrill cries new little refuse mounds grew up around the piles of pickings and all hell broke loose over the division of these mounds among the neighbourhoods and the hut people. People took their children there very early in the morning and did not go home until dark. The bits of plastic, iron, bottles and paper they gathered were sold to the nearby workshops, while all the time the trucks came to Flower Hill driving the pickers down to the stream away from the refuse. Every time the trucks arrived, the Flower Hill people ran to the stream and huddled together, but as soon as the trucks left they dispersed again among the refuse heaps. They were harried for days. Then one forenoon the garbage owner came to Flower Hill in his snow-white car and, holding a white handkerchief to his nose, he showed them sealed and stamped documents proving his rights.

After that morning the owner gave the Flower Hill people a little money per kilo for their pickings, and no more trucks came to the Hill to attack the scavengers. Instead of precious stones and pieces of gold, blood-red sores appeared on their hands. The children stole plastic baby dolls with broken legs and heads from the rubbish heap and played with them in secret. The women kept an eye open for the watchmen and thrust the cracked fancy mirrors they found into their pockets, and at night they looked in these mirrors and combed their hair with combs from the garbage. Flies from the refuse settled on their hair. With the mingled stench of refuse and factory, the wind blew continuously into the huts and into people's noses, so they sealed their doors and windows and ate bowlfuls of yoghurt to avoid being poisoned. At night they wore plastic sacks to escape the flies. Children were lost inside the bags; the adults drew up their knees and curled up into balls. Breathing holes were made for their mouths, but after midnight the sacks were like steaming clouds dripping hot tears.

Back in the village the community shepherd girls who used to milk the sheep that grazed out in the summer pastures at night were called 'Berji Girls' by the community who held the job of bringing in the milk and carrying it to the village in high esteem. A girl's upbringing was measured by the way she went about milking the sheep. A shepherd girl had her hair stroked and was called 'Dear

Berji girl'. On Flower Hill only the girls who picked over the refuse were considered worthy of the name and awarded such praise. A girl's reputation on Flower Hill was judged by whether she collected refuse or not, and by the way she went about her work.

When it became clear who the owner was the men gave up picking over the garbage and went off to find work and a living beyond the Hill. Collecting garbage was considered child's work, women's work. The women filled their pouches rapidly as though gathering herbs or sorting over cracked wheat. At the same time they minded their homes and children. The men went without work for days, for so long that they got into the habit of getting together to congratulate anyone who had found work, and a woman whose husband had found a job strutted proudly round all the huts, distributing halva and kissing hands. But those who had failed to get work turned this custom into something very different. The halva distributors were cornered behind doors by the other women, pinched black and blue, and eventually beaten up openly.

There was no lack of wind to tear the roofs off the shacks on Flower Hill. Holding on to roofs, wearing plastic sacks at night and washing in bluish hot water came to seem as natural as eating and drinking. And when the wind blew very hard the squatters climbed out on the roofs and lay down flat to stop them taking off. This was far more effective than pulling from below with ropes and hooks. Meanwhile 'stoning the wind' became a custom. For every roof climbed, a handful of radish seed was scattered below Wind-Curse Point and the wind was stoned to death.

But stoning the wind was useless. On the contrary, after every stoning it blew up even blacker and fiercer against the people. Sweeping straight down on the roofs it tore the pitchpaper off the ceilings and left it swinging loose. It lifted walls off the ground, caught women and children in the street and blew them over. No tears could wash away the dust swirled about by the wind. Heads were racked with pain, and over their floral headscarves the women tied thick bands of cloth called 'Windbreakers' round their aching heads. The men went about pressing their hands to their ringing ears. The trees on Flower Hill grew sideways instead of upwards, and the birds came and went, swooping over the hill.

While the wind blew in fits and starts the Flower Hill folk made up all kinds of wind stories. They believed the wind was the hill's lover who resented their coming and establishing a community up there and they thought if they adopted the wind's name, it would quieten down. They gave the name 'Wind' to children born at the time, whether they were male or female. They composed wind songs and even invented games about it.

The children forgot blind man's buff and hide-and-seek and discovered new games, mostly played sitting down. They stood before the wind and turned into whirligigs or, sitting on sheets of tin, flew down to the stream with outstretched arms, and they called this game 'Giving the Wind the slip'. The women carrying water on their backs produced other unsual games as they came and went. They walked from one hilltop to another swinging and splashing water from their cans. They knelt, then stood in a row and sang, *Water, water, pretty water! Droplet, flying droplet! Let the wind, my lover, come!*

The men invented a different game called 'Walking against the Wind'. They played it on Rubbish Road which joined the minibus route half an hour away from Flower Hill.

> *Oh Wind,*
> *My eyes keep running, my poor knees shake,*
> *All the time my shoulders ache,*
> *My arms can't lift, my fingers chill,*
> *One of us must leave this hill.*

The Flower Hill simit-sellers and pedlars made up the song. The factory workers on the Hill countered the Flower Hill folk by making up their own song and dance, in which the Flower Hill men also took part. Every morning they walked ten steps apart in a row, from one end of the road to the other, some facing, some back to back. First they began to sing all together, then with hunched backs and bowed heads and arms held stiffly by their sides, they compressed their shoulders and drew in their necks. When they reached the middle of the road they sang 'Hey, Wind, hey!' and all turned sideways on to the wind.

Surprisingly, this dance continued in the same order every morning and evening. When the factory night-shift had dispersed, the workers appeared at the gates in a row. They stood before the watchmen who searched their pockets to check if they had stolen anything from inside; after the search the workers came out on the road and began the wind dance. And before they got half-way down the road the hut people met them gliding slowly like black birds.

In time changes came about through the wind dance performed by the Flower Hill men on Rubbish Road. They became accustomed to walking sideways, hands pressed to their sides, bowing their heads as they walked. One winter day when the wind was flinging the snow over the shacks, they were completely bent double and that snowy night they came home with twisted backs and necks awry and fell into bed fevered and sweating. For ten days the Flower Hill men did not open their eyes from 'Wind Sickness'; then the fever and sweat stopped and the illness passed but left them with neck and shoulders even more twisted and lopsided.

The people of Flower Hill resorted to unheard-of remedies to try and heal the distortions caused by Wind Sickness. The women strapped their husbands to bedsteads and divans with stout ropes, but when the ropes were loosened the muscles of their knees and necks collapsed. Their spines caved in, flaccid as dough. For days on end men lined up at the bonesetters' doors. There were men in plaster, men with their backs tied to wooden planks, and men with their necks encased in metal hoops.

These incurable distortions opened the way for endless debate on Flower Hill; a different suggestion issued from every throat. The women left off singing the water song and every day they keened a different lament, 'Backs are bent in bandages of wood; necks are aching, knees don't hold.' Holding their stooping backs, the men walked sideways to the coal depot and gathered by the stove. They looked for a cure for their condition, but however much they talked around the problem they arrived only at a dead-end. Yet the debate went on and on. Some said the remedy was to have a bus service, and they made written applications at the coal depot, some signing with names and some with fingerprints. Then, with their sideways walk, they took their applications to an official building. But no bus service came. Some said it had come but gone back because of the mud on Flower Hill, or that the wind had stopped it. Dreams and twitching eyes were regarded as good omens for the bus service. Woollen bandages were wound round the necks and backs of the men as they all watched the road. When the bandages were undone, smoke from the stoves was applied to their contortions and steam to their necks and backs. The steam rose and a cloud formed. After the snow, rain fell on the settlement for days. Water dripped into the huts, and in the dripping rain which dissolved and crumbled the walls the twisted necks of the Flower Hill men and the tearful eyes of the women remained unchanged. The women waited for days on end at the gates of the chemical factory but the deathly-white pills they got from the workers were useless.

As the white pills were no good they followed the advice of the oldest bedridden woman in the community. At the beginning of spring they gathered to pray. They took their husbands' underwear and the bandages that had been wrapped round their backs and necks and climbed up to Wind-Curse Point where they heaped up the bandages and clothes, set fire to them and circled round the fire. At each circling they beat their breasts, invoking 'My lord of the black eyebrows and tapering moustache' and prayed to God to remove their husbands' deformities. The bandages and underwear burned to ash and the women took hope from Wind-Curse Point and went back home where they waited for days sitting by their husbands. But the prayer for a cure was not heard and did not work. With their deformed necks and backs, the men who had been ill that spring were unable to keep their jobs. The simit-trays and lemon boxes stood empty in the gardens, construction builders were turned away in ones and twos from the building sites. Every day they met and turned up at the gate of a different factory, holding their heads as upright as they could. They stuck their hands in their pockets and secretly straightened their backs but with their weakened spines and wilting necks they could find no work at the factories.

At the time the men of Flower Hill were struggling to find work, a shiny blue sign — 'Nato Avenue' — was hung on the wall of one of the chocolate factories up Rubbish Road. United by curiosity they marched with their sideways walk until they arrived under the street sign, but as they could not figure out what the writing on it stood for or why it had been put up, they turned back. They were quite pleased, but after lengthy discussions they decided this road could not possibly be an 'avenue'. Some said an avenue must be made of asphalt and some insisted that asphalt had nothing to do with it, but a road could only be called an avenue if it had rows of apartment blocks or trees planted on both sides. Others suggested that an avenue must have buses and taxis. Two other people recovering from Wind Sickness thought the street sign was a good omen — it meant that Flower Hill would soon have water, buses and electricity. Discussions went on, and they finished up by speculating on the meaning of 'Nato'. Some said that once upon a time the papers had written about Nato, and others that the radio played folk songs from Nato. One said it meant 'Armed Force', another, 'Bombing'. The hut people were upset by this talk of arms and bombs and did not warm to the name. They came in a body to Güllü Baba's place. He listened in silence. In his own mind he attributed the deformity of the Flower Hill men to the erection of the street sign. He struck the ground with his stick again and again and asked, 'Can it possibly be that Nato has some connection with deformity?'

Once Güllü Baba had suggested this, the hearts of the Flower Hill people trembled and all kinds of ideas were put forward. Some made guesses about the men who had put up the street sign, where they came from and where they'd sneaked off to; some asked what business was it of anyone whether they were deformed or not. They swore, and the women raged at the wind and the street sign. Some people wanted to know in what language 'Nato' meant 'deformity' and others were obsessed by the question of why the sign didn't simply say 'deformity'. In the end the whole matter reached an impasse. Those who said 'Nato' had no connection with 'deformity' and who had come out and explained to everyone that it was a 'big institution' to do with the state, fell silent. And one night the men and women of Flower Hill took down the street sign and threw it over Wind-Curse Point. The women returned to their huts cursing and the men assembled and kissed Güllü Baba's hand.

Güllü Baba's stick touched the backs of those who kissed his hand. Head in hand, he sank muttering into the depths of his wisdom. He introduced the subject of the pockets of 'language-cells' in the right side of the head — and to these he attributed the fact that Nato Avenue could not survive as a name. He explained that it was impossible to erase the name Rubbish Road from the minds of the Flower Hill dwellers. After Güllü Baba's explanation, the name of the road remained always Rubbish Road in the settlers' language-pockets.

Before he got the Wind Sickness Güllü Baba had worked in a little biscuit factory. Being blind in both eyes he had used his stick to take part in the walking game against the wind on Rubbish Road. His rise to the rank of spiritual guide on Flower Hill had come about when trembling and in tears he had cured Sırma. From then on there was discussion for days on end among the women in the settlement as to whether anyone who was blind could weep or not, and eventually, it was decided that the tears which flowed from his blind eyes were a powerful and holy water. Rumours were rife that God regretted making him blind, that He had asked him whether or not he wanted eyes, and that Güllü Baba had asked for a powerful mind instead of eyes. His knowledge of things unknown to anyone else was attributed to his blindness. As more and more people witnessed him talking with his stick and listening to the earth, no work in the neighbourhood was undertaken until Güllü Baba's hand had been kissed. They believed that the Bird of Luck would perch on the head of anyone touched three times on the back by Güllü Baba's stick.

The stick was the same age as Güllü Baba's blindness. While he was working on a dam construction job he had fallen from a height and lost his sight. There was a song composed by Güllü Baba himself about his blindness which everyone on Flower Hill knew, but Güllü Baba sang it best of all.

> *The eye's the mirror of the soul, it's said,*
> *My soul is many-coloured, my eyes dead,*
> *I broke my mirror in a fall.*
> *No use at all!*

Güllü Baba made various predictions about the future of Flower Hill. They were so mysterious that nobody could understand them. He said that one day the earth would form a crust over the garbage hills and new huts would be raised on the garbage, and flowers of all colours would spring up around the huts. And even inside the huts green, green grass would sprout. According to him, the tins and bottles and bits of plastic which gleamed under the brilliant green grass on both slopes of the refuse would bring crowds to Flower Hill to look at the iridescent effects of these hills, and at the huts where grass and flowers sprang up inside. He said that the huts on Flower Hill would multiply even more, and the wind would lose its former strength but would carry sounds from ear to ear and hut to hut. Whenever a group of women in need of water knocked on his door he muttered to his stick, listened to the earth and announced that eventually water would be found at the end of a long road. He advised the women who came with their newborn babies, asking for his blessing and kissing his hand, to bury shrivelled umbilical cords in the factory gardens. This, he said, would help their children find work in the factories when they grew up.

So they secretly buried in the factory grounds the dried-up umbilical cords of the children born on Flower Hill and offered prayers that when they grew up they would not be unemployed. People of ambition buried their babies' cords in the gardens of workshops and repair shops, in the hope that their children would learn a craft. Some even took them to the garden of a distant school. Morning and evening, men kissed Güllü Baba's bramble-stained stick to find work. And the women brought him their sick children with headaches and fevers and running eyes and noses. Güllü Baba, pouring tears and listening to the earth, sent up an aches-and-pains prayer every day. He recited his prayers and blew on the aching heads and eyes and ears of the children who knelt before him. He touched their backs three times with his stick. *Song and Custom*

> *O Rose-stick, set the eyes aright,*
> *Dry up the ears that weep,*
> *Bring comfort with your healing touch*
> *And lull this child to sleep.*

Summer came with all sorts of trouble and new kinds of sores and the frequent kissing wore away the rosewood stick. The bramble dye and violet colour rubbed off, and the thin shaft was bent and its handle crooked like the necks of the Flower Hill men. Moreover, its power was affected by the factory waste and gradually it began to confuse squinting eyes with fainting fits brought on by chemicals, and squinting eyes with the stifling effects from the garbage. Eventually the stick completely lost its power to cure fevers by making sweat pour, and aches and pains by calling up a wind to blow them away. It had become an insignificant yellow wand which slipped off their backs and was no longer spoken of or respected by the Flower Hill folk. Only one saying remained from the purple stick which they alone understood — '*My troubles fade with bramble-dye.*'

As the factory waste eroded and undermined the stick's power, Flower Hill transferred all its hopes to the waters of wisdom shed from Güllü Baba's eyes. Güllü Baba put forward all sorts of views on the factories, the wind, the garbage and unemployment. He listened to the earth and wept unceasingly for water, for work and for the cure of the illnesses spread by the garbage and the factory waste. For a long time his torrents of tears made up for the weakness of his stick. But gradually the tears which had streamed so rapidly at first became harder to shed. He grew deaf to the sounds of moaning women on their knees before him, children yelling in pain, and men writhing and pleading for work. His callused hands lost their sensitivity to fever and trembling. To produce a single tear he had to squeeze his eyes shut for a long time, moaning and struggling to fill his heart with grief, and when his last two teardrops had been shed for Şengül to make her milk flow, Flower Hill was deprived of the water of wisdom.

When they brought Şengül to Güllü Baba, two bags of mint were tied over her breasts which were completely filled and clogged with milk. For ten days milk oozed into her breasts, while pain spread from her armpits, and her shoulders sagged from the weight. Her face turned blue from pain, then reddened, then paled, and she moaned interminably in a high quavering voice. Besides Şengül,

there were two women with 'problems of bleeding' and a
little girl who wanted Güllü Baba's tears. For a long time
Güllü Baba's heart had not been deeply touched but
Şengül's cries moved him far more than the others' shouting. 'When I cry my tears belong to everyone,' he said as he
set her by his knees. Şengül looked into his face hopefully,
then unbuttoned her blouse and quietly told him her age,
her name, and her husband's name. She kissed Güllü
Baba's hand, and he felt for her right breast and held it. He
gave her one of his hands and told her to bite it if she could
not stand the pain. He squeezed her right breast as hard as
he could, and Şengül's eyes filled with tears, blood streaming from her breast. She collapsed on the ground. Then
Güllü Baba quietly took from his pocket a fine-toothed
plastic comb and knelt by her. For a long long time he
stroked her breast with the comb and passed his hands over
her. He breathed a prayer from his heart, and with
difficulty he made out Şengül's face as she lay fainting on
the ground — her shapely mouth, her black curved eyebrows and lashes sweeping her cheek. Lost in thought,
Güllü Baba moved his hands over her milk-filled breasts,
and then two teardrops fell from his eyes. 'Let me waken
your milk, my little quail, so you may wake up too', he said.
He sighed and shook Şengül gently. Still stroking and
praying he opened her eyes. He advised her to bind her
breasts with rose petals when the moon came up that night;
and when the moon was fading to loosen her hair and comb
both her hair and breasts: he said that if the milk flowed
and her baby still didn't suckle, she should steal another
baby's swaddling clothes, burn them at midnight, and hold
her breasts to the smoke. She kissed his hand again,
buttoned up her blouse and picked up her baby. That night
when the moon rose she wrapped her breasts in rose petals
and when it faded she freed her hair and combed her hair

and breasts. She stole swaddling clothes and burned them but instead of milk, blood poured from her breasts and open sores appeared.

Şengül's lament reached the sky over Flower Hill. Those who were pained by it came knocking at her door, some recommending a mixture of dough and pepper to be slapped on the breasts, others to pound down Turkish delight and apply it. They shed tears for Şengül's breasts and beat their bosoms. She showed her breasts hopefully to every comer and let everyone handle them, until they were nearly ready to drop off. Then Mother Kibriye came staggering to the rescue and said, 'If you can find me some silver thread I'll turn them into weeping brides.' She swore she'd cure them. She told the women that she knew where everything was in the body, and she recited the names of the complete anatomy of the chest and the base of the neck. Soon, she promised, there wouldn't be a single infertile woman left on Flower Hill; she would distribute prescriptions to the women suffering from exhaustion and loss of blood which would cure them like magic! For years she had been soothing the lovesick hearts of the young with seeds and herbs and relieving their pains, and getting rid of unwanted children. After listing all her skills, she told the story of how a torrent had carried herself and her seven children to Flower Hill. Before dealing with Şengül's breasts, she made the women cry as she described the spouting foam and the water reaching the sky and, while they were all in tears, the silver thread was found. Mother Kibriye dried her eyes on her yashmak and sat down in front of Şengül. She mixed dough in a bowl, cut the silver thread in tiny pieces and stuck them on the nipples with the dough. The bosom shone. She blackened her finger with soot from the pots and drew a huge eyebrow and eye on each breast: she drew lashes for the eyes. Şengül was breathless with pain, but Mother Kibriye stroked her hair and whispered in her ear, 'Now you're a bride, you're a bride, now you can cry.' Quickly with a razor she cut first one breast then the other. And tears of blood flowed from the cheeks of the two brides who gazed from Şengül's full bosom. And when the brides wept Şengül was at peace, her heart relieved.

Before the open wounds on the brides' 'faces' had closed, Flower Hill re-echoed with the news that Güllü Baba's eyes had dried up. Şengül was nicknamed 'The Bride Who Dried up the Tears'. All the women who had come to Flower Hill to admire her beauty and weep for her breasts turned hostile when they heard that Güllü Baba shed no more tears. They cursed her beauty, and every time they saw her they turned their backs and slapped their rumps. Children banged tins at her door, and the men prowled round her furtively.

After the Flower Hill folk had given up mourning, they waited for Güllü Baba's tears to flow again. The women gathered at his door. They cooked him broths which they made him drink, saying,'May they bring tears and grief.' Every now and then they brought him Sırma and put her hands into his withered ones. But Sırma grew tired of coming to Güllü Baba, and she began to stamp her foot and cry. The women made her sprinkle water on his face and they smeared her tears on his eyes, but however much he tried to grieve he couldn't manage a single tear. His spirit exhausted, his power gone, he fell ill. Tossing and turning in his bed, he repeated, 'The factories are howling', and as he tossed he made new guesses about Flower Hill. He gave away Flower Hill's secrets to anyone who came to visit him.

Güllü Baba had come by these secrets through his tears.

God had dried up his tears, but had bestowed another gift of priceless value in their place which was the ability to discover secrets known only to Him. Through this gift he could foresee the fate of the Flower Hill folk: on their foreheads were inscribed, in deep black letters, factories, wind and garbage. These would be the bringers of good luck and bad; factories would be opened on Flower Hill where the deformed men would work, and there would be so many more factories that the women and children would stop scavenging and would fill them: the community would prosper, but their sores would never heal. The factory waste would alter the colour of the earth, the howling wind would scatter, and murmurs would turn into screams.

Güllü Baba, throughout his illness, turned Flower Hill upside-down by giving away many of its secrets. Along with the factories, the garbage and the wind, his name was inscribed on Flower Hill in deep black letters through his predictions, his advice and the words uttered in his sleep. After his recent accounts people began to look with apprehension at the garbage trucks as they came and went, the collectors in their black aprons, and the factories and garbage hills. They saw the wind as having magical powers and gave up the custom of 'stoning the wind'. It was replaced by the custom of giving ear to the wind, listening to its howling and waiting for the sounds it carried. Güllü Baba left off reciting prayers and breathing on their sores and began to tell fortunes in return for cheese, olives and soup. He no longer talked about the many different colours of flowers which would bloom on the garbage hills, and the huts in which bright green herbs would flourish. The prayers and laments he had raised were forgotten, erased from ear and memory, replaced in Flower Hill idiom by Güllü Baba's poetic metaphors, such as 'My troubles are greater than the mountains of garbage,' 'The factories howl,' 'My eye, like a young girl's, lights on work, food and water.' As the factories howled, and the garbage mountains grew in height, new gnomic sayings were added. The factory noise, howling wind and stinking garbage became an insoluble problem, an inaccessible mystery. Factories, waste and garbage crept into the Flower Hill songs alongside the wind: the cranes took wing, and the deer stole away. On Flower Hill, young people in love would complain, 'My heart is ravaged like the mountains of garbage.' A cloud settled on the factories, snow flaked over the huts. The screams of the sea birds filled the Flower Hill sky; waste matter spoiled the earth, and the earth colour turned red while the blue plaster on the hut-walls rotted away.

> *Tell your name, O Falcon-lad!*
> *Peregrine Doğan.*
> *Who's your father?*
> *I'm the son of Garbage Grocer.*
> *Is your love a shepherd maid?*

While Güllü Baba was predicting the future for the Flower Hill people, the Nato Avenue sign was put up again, shiny and blue, on the chocolate factory wall up Rubbish Road. On the same day the bluish hot water was cut off, and factory snow stopped falling on the huts. A huge tent was pitched in front of the chemical factory, and over the door hung a red banner announcing Workers' Strike. A worker grabbed a big tin can and whirling round and round began to drum and sing:

> *Ding Ding, Dinga Ding,*
> *Out on strike the chemists went,*
> *Keep it going, Dinga Ding,*
> *By the factory bloomed a snow-white tent.*
> *Keep it going, Dinga Ding.*

The banging echoed back and forth between the factories, and all the strikers joined in the singing until their quavering voices reached the hills and huts.

When factories on Rubbish Road went on strike, and the tent was pitched and the banners hung up, this banging and singing became a habit. The workers called it 'The Strikers' Song'. It originated from the first strike in Rubbish Road when the women who worked on the dry batteries used to sing, 'A white tent, the rose of Rubbish Road, an ill wind, the wind of Rubbish Road.' After them came the linen workers who put up their strike banner and let the wind blow the rose of the song away while they danced a folk dance shoulder to shoulder in Rubbish Road. The wind seized their tent and whirled it to the skies, then it fell into the garden of the factory which made batteries for cars.

> *By the factory bloomed a snow-white tent,*
> *Keep it going, Dinga Ding,*
> *But the wind blew up and away it went.*
> *Keep it going, Dinga Ding.*

Leaving the tent in the garden it circled round Flower Hill where it blew and blew. After Flower Hill was founded the first to strike were the chemical workers. The noises which filled the women's buckets by the hot water fountain overflowed into the streets of Flower Hill, stirring up alarm and confusion; children left off playing and scavenging for garbage; men came bent and stooping out of their doorways; women took up their babies; everyone went to watch. Not a soul was left in the huts.

> *Out on strike the chemists went*
> *Keep it going, Dinga Ding,*
> *To the lightbulb men they sold the tent.*
> *Keep it going, Dinga Ding.*

Passing on the tent was a Rubbish Road custom which dated from the strike in the car battery factory. The arrival of the linen workers' tent in the garden of the car battery factory meant that it would be the next to strike. And so it came about, before the linen workers had time to dismantle their tent and go back to work. The battery workers pegged down their tent securely and on the first day sent a white pigeon flying off to a round of applause. The bird shot into the sky like an arrow and was lost in the smoke of the factories of Rubbish Road. Then it circled round and perched on top of their factory. That turned out to be the longest strike on Rubbish Road. Snow fell on their tent; frost came. After the rains came summer. The strike banner lost its colour and the writing faded. Then the workers who had flown the pigeon and danced side by side to keep their tent from blowing away, disappeared one by one from their place by the tent. Only a handful of men remained at the factory gate. The stubborn ones who stood fast were called 'Tent Stewards' by the others.

Afterwards the Tent Stewards were dismissed and 'New Blood' workers were taken on at the car battery factory. The strikers with lead poisoning went off down Rubbish Road and kept looking back until they were out of sight. The name 'Tent Steward' was left behind as a reminder to the workers on the road. After that strike, anyone who called a meeting in the factory changing-rooms, or in the toilets or picket lines and spoke of exploitation and the existence of a working class, was known as Tent Steward. Like raising the tent, the banner and the song, it became the custom to fly pigeons during strikes and they believed that the factory where the pigeon settled on a roof or chimney would have the next strike. The workers of that factory would be called out with shouts and applause, and while they were all dancing, the strikers' tent would be passed on to the workers of the factory elected by the pigeon.

> The white dove swooped on the lightbulb.
> Were her wings empty or laden?
> Laden! Oh laden!
> With what was she laden?
> With yoghurt and gifts
> Of tobacco and sugar
> And packets of tea!

The chemical workers gave their tent away to the workers of the lightbulb factory and their banner — 'We Support You' — was hung on the factory wall. There was a united shout of 'Long Live Strikes!'. Then they lined up shoulder to shoulder to dance. The men of Flower Hill joined in too, shaking their shoulders. The children clapped, the women pointed at the dancing women workers and giggled and pinched one another.

Holding a white kerchief, Kara Hasan sprang from the line of dancers into the middle. With outstretched arms and bent knees, he started up a song about having his white horse shod. Gradually the song grew faint, high-pitched and breathless. Then Kara Hasan dropped his head on his twisted neck and slapping his hands on the soles of his feet whirled round and round, in ecstasy. The others had stopped dancing and everyone in Rubbish Road came to watch. Kara Hasan waved his kerchief and wriggled his shoulders until his shirt was stained with sweat. The more he danced the more he enjoyed it. And when he finally dropped back among the Flower Hill folk to general applause, he could not help dashing back to his hut where he looped wire round his ears and attached animal skins to his back and front. He came back to the picket line with a thin stick in his hand and began to dance again, swinging and dangling the animal hides. The entire Rubbish Road was on its feet. As he leapt about, the strikers watched and guffawed, and the Flower Hill folk clapped their hands. His stick lunged at the strikers and squatters, he rolled over and over on the ground and then took off the skins and spread them out on the picket line. He did not leave his place by the tent until the chemical workers went back to work.

While Kara Hasan was sitting by the tent with wires round his ears, all kinds of rumours were circulating through the Flower Hill community. On the first day of the strike the story spread that a sacrificial sheep was slaughtered at the tent door and its meat distributed as 'The Chemical Workers' Tool'. According to those who went to pray at the Flower Hill mosque with the tin minaret, the sacrifice was intended as an offering by the chemical workers to the Union. Most of the workers in Rubbish Road had hastened to join the Union, but the chemical workers could not make up their minds though they had meetings at night in their homes and by day in the coffee houses on Rubbish Road. They had been described as 'Tool-less' for not belonging to the Union, and they took the insult hard — it likened them to impotent husbands. So they distributed sacrificial meat as the 'tool' of their work-force and shouted and danced, their foreheads smeared with the blood of the sheep.

This story was mixed up with nasty rumours about why the hot water fountain had gone dry. Many cursed the workers for raising such a hue and cry, banging tin cans and flying pigeons, and others said that this was not the proper way to go out on strike. Then they heard that the Union would hire drummers and zurna players to play music for the strikers for three days and nights in Rubbish Road. When they heard this the Flower Hill folk were full of curiosity and began to argue about whether there was a place for music in a strike. The argument developed when some queried the reason for the strike in the first place and came to a head when they asked why people were constantly coming and going to the picket line carrying bits of cloth with writing on them. Some thought it was due to the sacrificial rite; those who had wishes they wanted fulfilled wrote them on the cloth which they had brought to hang up at the picket line. They had particular hopes and expectations from the tent and the sacrifice. Others believed that those who came were supporters of the strike who would still have come even if no sheep was slaughtered and no pigeon flown. The Union's orders were that all its members should have support in a strike, and the tent and the pigeon were also subject to the Union. While everyone was asking one another what 'The Union' (sendika) meant, Güllü Baba explained that the name derived from the word 'box' (sandık). He told the Flower Hill folk, when they came to have their fortunes told, that where he used to work there were certain boxes into which the workers would cast bits of paper on which they had written their wishes and desires. He said that money was paid from these boxes for those who got married, or were bereaved, or who had an arm or leg caught in the machines. Güllü Baba's explanations put the lid on the nasty rumours about why the hot water fountain had gone dry. The wishes of the Flower Hill folk were written on a piece of cloth, and the men and women of Flower Hill paid a visit to the picket line, with Güllü Baba in the lead. Flour, lentils and cracked wheat were collected

from the households and given to the strikers and after reciting a prayer before the tent, Güllü Baba told the fortune of the strike, saying there was light at the beginning and end of it. He interpreted the dreams of the workers around him and foretold the future of Rubbish Road. Then in return for the breath and energy spent he asked that the banner bearing their wishes be hung in the right-hand corner of the picket line. The banner with the Flower Hill wishes was hung according to his request and remained at the factory entrance, adorning the picket line, until the last day of the strike.

> *The downy dove,*
> *The strike-tent's pole,*
> *Water to drink*
> *Is Flower Hill's goal.*

The hut people wrote long strings of verse in crooked writing expressing their wishes for work, roads, buses and schools. Dancing about in his animal skins, Kara Hasan recited these to music for all who came and went on the picket line. And he developed a new skill. Cupping his hands round his nose he began to imitate the melancholy notes of a zurna mourning the hut people's troubles. He composed a song about their sufferings during the founding of the community, and about the roofs and cradles which flew away, and the snow which fell on the babies; it made the Rubbish Road workers weep. When he saw their tears Kara Hasan abandoned his skins and his white horse act. He removed the wires from his ears, and by listening to the talk of the workers and union members he discovered the factories' secrets. He told the hut people about the moving conveyor belts, the drills that scattered sparks as they revolved, and the blades that cut through glass. He was quite beside himself when he described the machine that poured 'snow' on the huts.

For days this machine was the talk of Flower Hill. It was as high as the factory ceiling and multi-coloured powders were piled before it. Everyone heard of the machine that held forty hutfuls of powder and of the stink it produced in the factory, even fiercer than the smell it blew at the huts. In a single day the story spread to the three communities of how the men working at the machine fell headlong into the powders and passed out. Kara Hasan fell flat on his face and did an impression of them which shook the people so much they forgot about the children who had fainted on the garbage heaps. Many wept and went off their food; Kara Hasan consoled them saying that towels, soap and sugar were distributed every month to the workers, but their feelings erupted again when he went on to say that the blood of the young girl workers was mixed with the hot water. He made imaginary drawings of the electric boiler and showed them to the people. He spoke of bottles exploding in the girls' hands, causing streams of blood and cut and torn faces. He hunched from one hut to another, declaring the running hot water was half blood. He pointed out to the women the girl strikers with their cut faces, and took the hut people one by one to the picket line to talk to the workers who had passed out. About the same time, the Flower Hill folk heard that the workers of Rubbish Road were a 'class', and that the Union would appropriate the factories on their behalf. Rumour spread that the workers had a power that could shake the world, and after Kara Hasan had explained the writing on the picket line banners, an epidemic of stories broke out in the community along with legends about the factory owners, the songs and customs of the workers, and things unimaginable.

The workers named the factories after their effects; some

made the lungs collapse, some shrivelled the eye, some caused deafness, some made a woman barren. Their proverb for marriage between equals was 'A bride with dust in her lungs to the brave lad with lead in his blood'. The saying gained ground when one after another the young car battery workers married girls from the linen factory. Young men who had worked in the car battery factories for two or three years could contract lead-poisoning and become impotent and the only match they could find on Rubbish Road was with the pale wan linen workers.

This practice on Rubbish Road became as well known among the hut people as the sad story of a factory owner who adopted a child who turned out to be deaf and dumb. The story fascinated the hut people far more than Kara Hasan's impressions of fainting workers, or the drawings from his imagination. And when they looked at Rubbish Road they narrowed their eyes and stopped their ears and grieved for days for the factory owner who was so kind to a stranger's dumb child.

However, the clouds of grief over Flower Hill were dispersed by yellow leaflets in ant-like print which were left quietly one night at the hut doors. All night long they were blown about the streets by the whirling wind; they flew over roofs and stuck in the branches of trees and against windows. Playfully they curled and twisted like little kites in the wind as it drove them downstream. Just before daybreak the whine of the wind changed to a scream throughout Flower Hill.

> *Flower Hill Folk!*
> *Awake, awake!*
> *Three black shadows have I spied,*
> *One stood ten paces in the rear,*
> *One whistled clear,*

> *And one into the gardens stole*
> *To scatter leaflets everywhere.*
> *I blew them far and wide.*

The wind's voice mingled with the wails of children, and one by one heads peered from the huts. Together they bent curiously over the leaflets caught in the branches and stuck under their doors.

> *Flower Hill Folk!*
> *Support the strike!*

At first the yellow leaflets confused people. They speculated on the three black shadows. Some said the strikers had distributed the leaflets; some thought one of the shadows could be Kara Hasan. Others could not understand why the workers would leave such leaflets and still others wondered why they could not actually speak up instead of writing and why they had left the leaflets in the dead of night. Meanwhile the contents of the leaflets were on everyone's lips and changed from person to person. The yellow leaflets grew bigger and bigger and Flower Hill was drowned in waves of anger. Everyone began to ask who the three black shadows were, where they came from and what business they had distributing leaflets and advice. The men got together and advanced menacingly on the picket lines with the leaflets in their hands. Güllü Baba's hut over-flowed. Kara Hasan swore he had never touched a yellow leaflet in his life and that he had been asleep when the three black shadows sneaked into the gardens of the huts. He offered as proof the dream he had had that night about dancing with the animal skins. No one owned up to the three black shadows, and the men who had gone so threateningly to the picket lines came back.

While Flower Hill and the strikers drew apart in a hostile silence the white tent turned as yellow as the leaflets on the doorsteps. The banners hung up at the picket lines on the first day of the strike, 'We want festival presents for our children,' and 'Are we workers or slaves?' faded and became illegible. The banners drooped and collapsed and with them Flower Hill's demands disintegrated. Only a few snatches of song from Kara Hasan's moving tunes still rang in the people's ears. The clatter of backgammon reached Flower Hill from the picket line. Women sat around with their knitting and lacework, bored and depressed, and strikers lay down in the white tent and fell asleep. Talk veered towards the silent factory behind the white tent. The workers who had looked with joy at the lifeless factory buildings in the first days of the strike were now saddened and they yearned for the roar of the machines while their hands missed the feel of the shiny tinkling glass vessels. They kept imagining the movement of conveyor belts.

The leaves of the strike year have faded away,
O my heart's full of sorrow!

While the strikers were waiting to get back to work Güllü Baba's water predictions came true. As the girls on strike sat writing heartbreaking poems in their scrapbooks adorned with filmstars, a strange epidemic from the drinking water spread over Flower Hill. Red beak-like sores appeared on every face, big and little, and soon the sores had covered the whole body. The numbers dropped of those who came from Rubbish Road to the tin minaret mosque on Flower Hill, and the gap widened between the strikers and the hut people. Kara Hasan fixed his gaze on the distant strikers' tent and listened to ballads borne on the wind, while his sores were eating him away. And as the girls went on inscribing their verses under the eyes of the scrapbook filmstars, the ulcers began to suppurate. The babies of the community stopped growing, and the children curled up at the foot of the divans, holding their heads. The men turned to scarecrows, with running sores on their deformed necks and heads, and when they walked their heads drooped sideways. The birds fled from Flower Hill; the chickens refused food from the women; the trees shed their leaves. The fallen leaves covered up the songs and dreams which grew out of the strike, and a crust formed over the talk that spread from Rubbish Road to the huts.

The people of Flower Hill had nothing left to talk about, so Güllü Baba laid aside his oracles and thought up wise things to say about the importance of water to human life: he urged the Flower Hill men to find water, as man's wits depended on it. The men were wearing down the factory doors in their demand for water when Mother Kibriye, who knew every part of the body, vied with Güllü Baba's wisdom, saying,'Only God can survive without water.' Telling them that the liver and kidneys swim in water and that a human being's organs would shrivel without water, she instilled fear in their hearts. She announced that shedding tears was fatal, warned the women to stop their children urinating and then told the story of how she had fallen victim to the water's anger, losing her husband in a foaming torrent. With renewed grief she withdrew to her hut.

Combined with Güllü Baba's insistence that a man's wits required unpolluted water, her warnings shook the whole community. The panic-stricken people took up buckets and began to wait by far-off water pumps. But the owners chained up the pumps and put them under lock and key.

When this unpolluted water was padlocked, Fidan of Many Skills who gave the women of the community 'Evening Classes' in the arts of the bed, opened her rosebud mouth. She cursed the men's deformed necks and the women's long fluttering lashes which shaded their cheeks. Her curses ran on and she flounced fiercely out of her hut. The sores in her eyes and ears were so bad she didn't know what she was saying or doing. She asked the men how they would enjoy sex without water. She picked up stones and hurled them at the huts and shouted that they wouldn't be able to take their wives to bed. Her voice was hoarse from shouting. Seizing a tin she struck it hard again and again and, gathering around her all the people in the community, she led them down the hill, until the earth and sky throbbed with the din.

> *Fidan of Many Skills goes to the water*
> *Jumping and skipping,*
> *Banging and drumming,*
> *Breasts bouncing ahead.*

The hut people on the march for water raced behind Fidan like an avalanche of rocks until they reached the breeze-block yard and brick factory. The red-faced brick workers gazed at them through the lattice screens, and their whistles and catcalls mingled with the banging tins. Fidan fled from the whistles like a deer going down to drink. When she saw the workers waving she stopped and laughed and wriggled her shoulders. Coyly, she planted her hands on her hips. Obscene comments mingled with the whistles, but Fidan turned her back and slapped her rump. Those who thought the brick makers were jeering at their ulcers and deformities cursed their red faces and hooded heads and a fight broke out between the hut people and the brick makers on account of water. Many were soon curled up on the ground with wounded heads: screams rent the air: children cried and women yelled. Beginning to feel guilty, Fidan stood among the women fluttering her shoulders like a partridge, puffing and panting, until she lost her patience and threw herself in among the men, tin in hand, and catching one of the brick makers, hurled him to the ground and jumped on him. He grabbed her by the shoulders which had provoked the whistling, pulled up her skirt and stared at her flowery underpants. Fidan shook him off and got up, swearing. Foaming at the mouth she kicked him hard. He collapsed by the bricks, holding his head, and turned his dust-filled eyes up to the sky. 'Whore!' he shouted. Fidan turned white as a sheet at the insult, peeled off her underpants and tied them on his head.

For days the brick makers passed round Fidan's flowery underpants and composed verses to them. They were tied to a post in front of the screens and, in the name of water, they streamed and waved like a flag. From that day on, the long wide road from Flower Hill to the town hall took the name 'Panty Way' to commemorate Fidan's flowery underwear.

For the sake of water Fidan had donated her underwear to the road and her bouncing breasts to folk-song. But the water wagons waited for the end of the strike before going up Panty Way to climb Flower Hill. A day before the wagons arrived the white tent was dismantled and brought to the electric bulb factory with dancing and clapping. The chemical factory went back to work, and the machine with the forty hutfuls of coloured powders started up with a rumble. Once more the snow that made people faint and ill fell on Flower Hill, and blue water streamed from the warm fountain.

The blue water flowed and sparkled in front of the wagons that carried the drinking water to Flower Hill, and Fidan went from hut to hut, plucking eyebrows and cutting fringes. She told the women that lovemaking was the best way to shed sin and find relief from worry, and she stirred up mischief by suggesting that men were not the only ones to enjoy pleasure, a woman also could have pleasure from sleeping with her husband. Along with the wind and the garbage, her reputation and her night lessons left their mark on Flower Hill. Songs for her mingled with songs about wind and garbage and her night lessons were heard in other neighbourhoods, in the factories and workshops of Rubbish Road. Her coquettish ways of leading a man on with seductive looks and provocative gestures were the talk of the factory workshops and dressing-rooms. When she fluttered her shoulders like a partridge she filled the young men's sleep and dreams, but for every new thing the women learned from her they took a beating from their husbands. Her shoulders that invaded dreams and her wits that brought beatings on the women distracted the wind as it carried off the sounds of Flower Hill. Once seduced, the wind rushed from the factories down to Panty Way and sweeping off the flowery pants the brick makers had tied to a pole, tossed them up in the air and blew about crazily beneath the clouds, adding the heavy roar of the factories to the softly-falling snow. The snow stopped the stink of the garbage heaps and whitened the Flower Hill homes. At night the wind swooped over the white huts and reached the roof of Garbage Grocer's home as it stood like a bird with outspread wings.

Panting and groaning, Garbage Grocer cast eyes on his wife so passionately that the roaring wind stopped in its tracks and the snow softened and melted. He pointed to his sweating flesh and said he was on fire. 'Turn round, girl' he said, and begged her to relieve him. He promised a thousand things if only she would dry up his sweat and put out his raging fire; he would bring her fragrant soaps wrapped in shiny paper and creams in screwtop jars with mirrors. But Garbage Grocer's wife did not give herself for soap and cream; she refused to go to her husband and defending herself with Fidan's lessons, she cried, 'Have you no fear of God, you pimp!' She cursed loud and long and poured out a stream of complaints. She stood screaming in protest that for years he'd treated her like a lump of wood and she'd never had the slightest taste of pleasure. When Garbage Grocer began to insist that pleasure was a man's prerogative she set up a lament: her constant cramps and back-aches and the frequent loss of colour which turned her face white as plaster all came about because there was no sexual satisfaction in her life. With tears streaming down her face she gave him a list of all the women who had experienced pleasure in intercourse, had stopped having headaches and had even got rid of their kidney stones. She sulked and hung her head, then lay down on the divan curled up like a ball. The Grocer's blood boiled with rage and he sang over and over one of the songs composed for Fidan. He wiped his sweat away fanning the feverish fire in his breast. The flames leapt and crackled and spread outwards, burning up whatever they touched but not dying down. The Grocer could no longer withstand his lust and sidling up to his wife, ordered her shamelessly, 'Come on, girl, turn round!' His wife swore she would not play the sheep and as he groaned and moaned she pouted and shrugged and stubbornly declared, 'I won't'. The Grocer lost his head, grabbed her by the hair and told her to clear off back to her father's. At first she stood without budging in the middle of the hut. But when she saw the scorching fire flaming out of his eyes ready to consume her, she squatted down like a bird with drooping wings and agreed to turn round. The Grocer took his pleasure. He had cooled his sweat and damped the fire, but his wife's defiance sticking in his throat, he perched on the divan and ordered her to sing the song, 'I won't come, I won't go,' and to walk up and down the hut a hundred times. He swore he would beat her till the roof came down if she missed a single turn, and his right hand signalled her to begin. She pleaded plaintively, but he remained unmoved. There was nothing for it but to begin, and she raised her voice in song and walked back and forth in tears, while the Grocer watched her. The wind laughed to see the Grocer's wife bobbing to and fro in the hut. Laughing, it blew above the huts and could not help dancing to her lively singing until dawn came to the white streets of Flower Hill. That morning it spread the news of the Grocer's wife who had asked for pleasure from intercourse but was made to sing instead.

Garbage Grocer's aspiring heart rose higher than the stars in the night sky. Soon after he came to Flower Hill he had a roof built on his hut; it looked like a bird with open wings and he decorated it with tiles. While everyone talked of the colour of the tiles and their grooved shape, he ripped out his door and in its place put a huge door with an embossed lion's head on it. He took to bragging endlessly about his lion door. Some were annoyed by his bragging and began to enquire secretly where Garbage Grocer had bought it. After lengthy research Nylon Mustafa (nicknamed 'Thankless' when the Flower Hill community was first founded as he did not know how to thank God) discovered the secret of where Garbage Grocer got his door. He immediately bought a lion door, stuck it on his own hut and threw the old one in front of Garbage Grocer's to annoy him. This act of Nylon Mustafa's was so approved of by the Flower Hill folk that there was no room to sit in his hut that evening. From the next day on everyone on Flower Hill took to replacing their doors, and soon several door merchants appeared with trucks on Flower Hill. Into the trucks they had piled the brass-knockered, lion-headed outer doors from the old city mansions and big stone buildings which were being pulled down here and there, along with stained-glass inner doors or frosted-glass bathroom doors, and brought them all to Flower Hill. Everyone fancied an embossed door and a stained-glass door. The hut doors were dismantled and Flower Hill took on a historical air. The streets gloried in pomp and splendour, and the huts had surprising number sequences, like 92/1, 117.

A new business, 'Door Trade', emerged from the enthusiasm of the Flower Hill community for the old embossed doors. And from that day trucks loaded with old doors roamed around the squatter communities. Whenever a community was starting up on one of the city hills, harvests of doors were stored at the top. The doors of crumbling mansions and stone buildings had climbed the hills, and the reign of Garbage Grocer's lion-headed embossed door had ended.

While the huts were being fitted with embossed doors, Garbage Grocer shut himself up for a time. Then, after a long silence, he summoned the men of Flower Hill to a meeting in his shop. He announced that Flower Hill mosque was too far from where his father lived; and asked for a second mosque to be built nearer. He said he had come to an understanding with Garbage Owner that if they agreed to build a mosque he would distribute money to the houses to wash the bits of plastic rummaged from the refuse. He rejoiced that the job of refuse-washing would eradicate unemployment. But Garbage Grocer's request for a mosque met with opposition on Flower Hill and the news that he had come to an understanding with Garbage Owner led to comments he found intolerable. He was so furious that he enclosed the land facing his front door. He built a mosque with a brass-knockered door for his father and he planted a tin minaret in his garden, the height of two men, that shone when the sun caught it. When he planted the minaret, words passed between Garbage Grocer and the Flower Hill folk and whatever he said was exaggerated and taken the wrong way. Then competition set up. First of all, Nylon Mustafa built a mosque in front of his hut, the height of his father. He stuck a bent tin can on the top and called it a minaret, and he perched a star and crescent on the point of the minaret. Following Nylon Mustafa's example, a few more rebellious huts demanded mosques and they were joined by others complaining, 'What about our fathers!' In the other huts anger swelled against those who fooled about with mosques as though they were toys. But when the third mosque hut was built in the Garbage Pit neighbourhood the anger turned into a race which ran and ran until snow fell on Flower Hill. Thanks to Garbage Grocer's heart which was exalted as the stars, Flower Hill was endowed with seven mosque huts.

Snow came sifting and drifting from heaven and stopped them planting minarets in front of their huts. And along with the wind it forced the Flower Hill folk inside and shut their embossed doors on them. Its flakes were caught in the roaring wind and tossed away. The factory rejects turned to ice under the snow. Where the bluish hot water slipped past, a bluish vapour licked at the snow and swallowed it up. It tore off the white snow cover and dissolved it. Everywhere the seagulls screeched together with laughter and swarmed over the garbage hills, their cries stifled, as they buried their beaks in the refuse. The factory rumble turned into the growl of the giant who lived over the mountains in Liverman's stories.

*H*ere today, gone tomorrow
There were many men to follow

With the beginning of winter one of these men appeared on Flower Hill, a snowy scene surrounded by factories and garbage mounds. As well as clever Keloğlan and brave Beybörek he conjured up giantesses and rich merchants, wise old men and fairy folk and began telling his nightly tales to the people of Flower Hill. Before launching into his story he rolled his clicking tongue round his mouth and recited a long jingle, inspired by his trade as liver-seller at the stadium gates. Then he took up the 'Epic of the Livermen' and related the fortunes of a huge family who had been selling liver fries for seven generations. Seven times during the Epic the Livermen quarrelled and broke up, but each time they reunited. In the end they parted, never to come together again. The Livermen Epic began many many years ago at the foot of white, foam-like hills of salt merging with the clouds, and as it ended with the Livermen dispersed to the four corners of the earth, the

Flower Hill folk sighed and sobbed. The Epic was followed by Beybörek's relentless struggle with the merchants and the giantesses. After a breathtaking account lasting three nights, all about Beybörek's adventures, Liverman was firmly enthroned in the hearts of the hut people. Once he started the tale of Keloğlan, his name took precedence over Güllü Baba's, Kibriye Ana's and Garbage Grocer's. His stories even replaced Fidan's night lessons.

Liverman had four grown-up sons and two daughters. People talked about his wife rather than his daughters because of her enormous sagging hips. Before capturing the hearts of the Flower Hill folk, Liverman had been best known for the double pair of spectacles which he kept in his chest pocket, and for the pile of newspapers tucked under his arm when he made his regular appearance every evening on Flower Hill. Since no one on Flower Hill was as fond of newspapers as Liverman, they used to mock the way he read lying down in the middle of his hut. As soon as he reached his hut he would stretch out on the floor and spread out the papers like a huge rug. He picked at the seeds of a large dried sunflower by his side and read the papers, changing his spectacles every now and then. He lay motionless in the middle of the hut, breathing softly until he nodded off. Then he curled up under the papers and fell asleep. During the day he and his sons sold liver at the stadium gates he mentioned in his jingle, at the head of Rubbish Road and at the horse races. His sons donned white aprons like his and white puckered bonnets. On their way to work, each held a glass bowl in his right hand full of tiny pieces of liver that stared with demons' eyes at the Flower Hill children. As the children scattered to the garbage mounds Liverman would reach Rubbish Road, his sons following him in descending order. Rumours about Liverman's family ran rife in the huts on Flower Hill. One was about how they quarrelled and broke up every year and how they never managed to stay in any one place for longer than a winter. No one on Flower Hill knew the reason for the quarrels which made them leave their homes and disperse, nor was it known how they found one another again or where they reunited. They had lived for a while in each of the neighbourhoods in the area known as the city's garbage hills, including Flower Hill, but had quarrelled and fled from each one of them.

This rumour was strengthened by the squatters from other communities who came to Liverman's hut and knelt there for three nights to listen to the story of Beybörek. More and more people believed in the truth of the rumour as Liverman would always begin a new tale by first reciting the episode of the dispersal from the Livermen Epic. Everyone, young and old, began to look forward to the quarrel that would break out in Liverman's home. As they waited in anticipation of a fight, they heard that an election would be held for a headman of Flower Hill. Then the word spread that Liverman had announced he would stand as candidate with the blessing of his giantesses, merchants and wise old men. Next day they heard that Nylon Mustafa too would be leaving the privacy of his hut to stand in the election. As whispers raced from hut to hut, Garbage Grocer's aspiring heart took fire, and his eyes were clouded by the vision of headmanship. Taking a square sheet of paper, he wrote down the reasons why he thought he should be elected, and stuck it up on his shop window. So white was this paper that the snow felt envious.

> Worthy people of Flower Hill!
> Would he who sleeps on the floor of his hut under a pile of newspapers make you a good headman?

Would he who sells liver at the horse races make you a good headman?
A fellow who stands by the stadium gates until dark and keeps company with Keloğlan until morn?
Discriminating people of Flower Hill,
Would Nylon Mustafa make you a good headman?
A fellow who says 'Adam and Eve are the forbears of man but who are the forbears of dogs?'
Would he who kept watch at the building site of the chemical factory make you a good headman?

Ferat Karabacak the grocer,
your candidate for headman.

Following the Grocer's appeal to the people's critical faculties, Nylon Mustafa came out from his hut and knocked on the door of each and everyone who had laughed at him for saying that men who wanted to find out about the world must let their intelligence take its course. He reminded them that curiosity was controlled by of the mind. He began his election campaign by explaining that an enquiry about the forbears of dogs was a way of finding out about the world and, to convince the squatters of the agility of his mind, he gave examples of the range of his own enquiries. He also declared he couldn't work out why God wanted men to pray to Him when He had so many angels. When he saw what astonishment his words aroused in people he became quite pedantic and asked them if they knew that men had dealt a blow at the Prophet of God. He had always wondered why God had not protected His Prophet from blows. He announced that in his hut he kept a precious illustrated book that had everything in it about the ways of the world and he hinted that for a long time he had been close to discovering the secret of man. He said the path was open to those who went about meditating and told them how he had spent his childhood wondering whether people with green eyes saw the world green. He explained to the electorate that those who were curious were also soft-hearted, and that all habits were acquired in childhood. While on the one hand he delved deep into his memories, on the other he accused Garbage Grocer of being slow-witted. Flower Hill was filled to the brim with people who spent all day at the factory gates, in front of the stadium and on the streets. He swore he didn't know who could be expected to vote for the Grocer. The power of his intellect shook Flower Hill and his comments on Garbage Grocer sparked off much discussion among the hut people. Liverman, who had so far tried to keep his hold on their hearts with the help of Beybörek and Keloğlan, now came forward with new tales and wrestling stories. All those who had spent the day in discussion gathered in his hut in the evenings. 'When snow fell on Flower Hill and chimneys blazed' was how he began his speech for the headmanship. He switched from tales to wrestling stories, breaking off at the most exciting moment with the problems of Flower Hill, and he made his appeal to the electorate with spitfire eloquence.

While the people of Flower Hill lay down to sleep, relaxed by Liverman's tales but muddled by the multitude of Nylon Mustafa's enquiries about the world, Garbage Grocer held conversations in quiet corners with Garbage Owner. After a while the Grocer made his way among the squatters with plans of settlement and started talking about something called 'bureaucracy'. He announced he would go into bureaucracy when he was elected headman of Flower Hill and referred to the party and the flag, spreading the word that he would distribute title deeds for the huts. He talked about gleaming golden water taps in the homes, promising that Flower Hill would be flooded with lights, and that power lines would encircle the huts. He took Flower Hill by storm with his speech on bureaucracy and the settlement plans drawn up on purple paper.

Nylon Mustafa was alarmed when he saw people running towards the Grocer's hut and proclaimed that he was 'the candidate of the workers and watchmen with crooked necks'. But the Grocer was quick to corner Nylon Mustafa with God's angels and the blows at His Prophet. He kept saying Nylon Mustafa had let his mind run dry and spread the word that he denied God. Nylon Mustafa insisted that curiosity was not denial, that as a child he would sit by the rocks and wonder if the world was nothing but his village. But such words were in vain, and so were his efforts when he tried to prove that he was a soft-hearted candidate by describing how as a child he used to make hammocks and rock the baby goats in them. Nylon Mustafa was turned away from every door he knocked at. Leaving the people of Flower Hill to their own aspirations, their eyes dazzled by the gleam of bright yellow taps and their ears hearing nothing but the sound of running water, he retreated to his hut. He bent over his precious book with the illustrations and began to wonder why animals fed on each other. He was surprised that the snake would swallow a nestling. He tried to understand why God hadn't put the world in better order and set himself to think.

After Nylon Mustafa had withdrawn to his hut, Garbage Grocer revived the rumour that Liverman's family would quarrel and disperse. Relying on the knowledge he acquired from the papers as he ate sunflower seeds, and on the excitement of his wrestling stories, Liverman stood firm. Every evening he let his wrestlers come to rest at the most unexpected moments, saying 'so now let's hear what

Liverman's wife has to tell us', and passed the word to his spouse of the sagging hips. Facing the people of Flower Hill as they all sat sighing and panting in excitement, Liverman's wife said, 'We may quarrel and break up, but we always return and make peace with each other'. She then went on at great length about what a loving and devoted family they were. Although they split up every year, she boasted, they could never stay apart but rushed back to embrace one another because they could not stand separation. But breaking up and reuniting was not accepted as something to boast about on Flower Hill. Once it was confirmed by Liverman's family that they did quarrel and split up, it was thought disgraceful that they should boast about it too. What Liverman's wife said made the hut people laugh and his family were left on their own with their wise old men and sweaty wrestlers. Liverman stopped telling stories; Beybörek went to rest on the divan, holding his sword, and Keloğlan hung his head. Liverman's hut was buried in silence and, as the snow caressed the huts of Flower Hill, the silence grew more and more uneasy. Soon after, a fight broke out between Liverman's family and the rich merchants. All sorts of noises came from the hut, grumbles and screams mingled with shouts and curses, and one evening Liverman left his hut and went away, cursing and swearing. Then his sons and daughters took to the streets and finally Liverman's wife charged out of Flower Hill, beating her breast. For days nobody went near their hut, and the doors and windows stayed open.

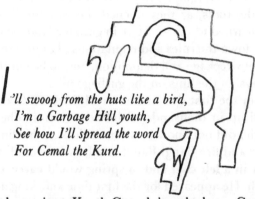

'll swoop from the huts like a bird,
I'm a Garbage Hill youth,
See how I'll spread the word
For Cemal the Kurd.

In the early spring, Kurd Cemal knocked on Garbage Grocer's door, now Garbage Chief, carrying a white-flowering branch as long as his arm and accompanied by two of his gunmen. The story went that the huts on the garbage hills were originally founded 'in Kurd Cemal's name'. He was the one responsible for the restless spreading of the huts. One morning he had come to the garbage heaps, far down Flower Hill at that time but now submerged under a rash of huts. The place was like a devil's lair; not a soul was to be seen but the truck drivers. Round about was pure desolation. As the early sun struck the mounds, Kurd Cemal could hardly see for the gleam and glitter of fragments of tin and broken glass. He compared the surrounding scene with his own village and wept, and when he had wiped away his tears which dripped on the glitter and mingled with the water trickling down the garbage, he established his authority on the slope. He divided up all the neighbouring land into plots and sold them. After the wrecking of the original huts had stopped, one by one he gathered the young layabouts who wandered aimlessly about the huts and distributed knuckledusters, money and guns. The young fellows called themselves 'Pot Belly' and 'Dragon'. They were swift as seabirds swooping from the roofs, as they opened the way for Kurd Cemal. They learned to say — 'Here in garbage land we're the ones to lay down the rules and regulations'. Gunfire replaced the noise of wreckage and demolition, and so began the 'Youthful Days' of the huts on the garbage hills.

From the first day of Flower Hill, Kurd Cemal's name turned up in thousands of different stories. There was no one who did not know how he would keep his finger on the trigger and fire Bang! Bang! and how he would dress up in winter in a felt coat and in spring would carry a flowering branch. He appeared for the first time knocking at Garbage Chief's door and Garbage Chief humbled himself and stood up to meet him. But while Kurd Cemal and his henchmen were deep in conversation with Garbage Chief, the people of Flower Hill suddenly rose in a body and poured into the street. When they heard that Kurd Cemal was to become a member of the Town Council they came running up, and the unemployed formed into a long line. The women with their water cans made a circle round Garbage Chief's red-tiled hut and forced Kurd Cemal to stop beside the water tankers. To rouse his sympathy they pretended to pick a quarrel and tore at each other's hair and faces. Kurd Cemal applauded them as they made this show of beating each other up. He announced his wish that Flower Hill be given shining new water taps as soon as possible. He promised the men who stood in his way asking for work in the factories that he would find them jobs when he joined the Town Council. Then he and his men marched along Panty Way and, as they disappeared from sight, Garbage Chief's front door, garden and hut interior filled with people. But Garbage Chief was silent, his lips sealed with a mouthful of concrete, and not a word of his conversation with Kurd Cemal leaked out. All the same, Kurd Cemal's comings and goings on Flower Hill turned into a rumour that he would open a cinema in the middle of the garbage hills.

But Kurd Cemal was on the point of opening up a brand new squatters' quarter, not in the middle of the garbage hills but where they ended. Finding a way round bureaucracy, he promised Garbage Chief money and land for a single hut and asked him to spread the news in the factories and workshops of Rubbish Road that the forest land beyond the garbage hills was being turned into heath, but to say not a word to the Flower Hill folk. While Flower Hill was approving velvet curtains and black leather armchairs for Kurd Cemal's cinema, Garbage Chief was going the rounds of the factories and workshops of Rubbish Road. 'Anyone who wants can become a hut owner here', he said, whispering Kurd Cemal's name in the ear of the workers who wanted to own a hut. Then he sold building plots in Kurd Cemal's name.

One night the workers left the factory and scattered to the forest land behind the garbage hills; they dug up the heath and levelled the earth. Then they set up random huts from breezeblocks. Four days later they were completely surrounded by menacing trucks and behind the garbage hills, that 'film' ran for days in Kurd Cemal's 'cinema'.

Welcome huts
Good riddance trucks

While the glittering screen of the garbage hills showed the smiling faces of weary workers, the cement dust stopping up Garbage Chief's mouth blew away through the streets of Flower Hill, and they heard how he had taken money from the workers. The people laughed for days at their own innocence and henceforth all such swindles were known as 'Kurd Cemal's Cinema', a name which spread to other neighbourhoods and factories. Tricks were played so thick and fast it became a byword and soon the name 'garbage hill' was forgotten among the hut people and replaced by 'Kurd Cemal's Cinema'. In that cinema, days merged with darkness, darkness with the moon, the moon with the stars.

Spring passed into summer.

Şerme, Şerme! Wakey wakey!
Rust-stained face
And sweatcloth ready.
Şerme, Şerme! Wakey wakey!

When the foreman of the nightshift appeared in the corridor of the refrigerator factory, the workers used to shout a warning, 'Şerme! Şerme!' so no one would be caught napping. They would throw bits of tin at any sleeping worker and make a noise to wake him up.

For Bald Ali these noises in the assembly line which could make a sleeper miss a heartbeat and jolt him awake to the conveyor belt were no more than a blanket. So he never woke up to the yells of 'Şerme! Şerme!' When the foreman shook him by the shoulders, he stretched out his feet against the wall and buried his head among the sacks. He thrust his bent elbow at the foreman, who took his card number to file a report. Then, after making a silent tour of the assembly line, the foreman stood by one of the workers who was hanging components on the conveyor and checked his speed by his watch. When he saw drops of sweat dripping on the conveyor belt from the cloths round the workers' necks, he pursed his lips, afraid he might be tempted to say 'take it easy', and hurried out. After he had gone, swearing and laughter broke out along the sliding conveyor belt. One of the workers picked up a longish wire, tied a rag on one end and dipped it in turpentine. It was a tail for Bald Ali, which he lit with a match, hooked on, then slipped away. Ali caught fire and fell on the floor, his clothes smouldering. 'Fuck you all!' he shouted aflame. Breathless, he tore off his shirt and trousers and stood stark naked. He bit his hand in fury and as he explored his hurts he began to cry.

> *Hairless Ali, don't you cry;*
> *We'll sling you on the old conveyor*
> *And treat your burns with dry hot air.*

The workers on the assembly line used to sing the 'Bald Ali' song as they placed components on the conveyor belt and it was such a lively tune that the 'evap' on the conveyor belt would dance as it was pushed along from one worker to the next. While Ali melted away in the heat that flamed in his face from the mouth of the furnace, the rest of the workers on the assembly line would roll his wiry body into a ball. As the nightshift foreman caught him napping every four or five nights, they used to call him 'Sleeping Queen, Song of the Assembly Line' and handle his head, his arms and legs, touching him up suggestively. Sometimes Ali would shrug and stay quiet, but sometimes he would snatch up a hammer and start chasing one of the workers, yelling 'Hey, hey!' 'There goes our Hey, hey Ali' they would laugh. Ali would spit curses at his tormentors, but the heat of the furnace and the noise of the sliding belt would stifle them.

The first huts to go up on the garbage hills were also the first to sing about Bald Ali before he became the subject of the workers' song. He used to sell well-water in tin cans on a donkey with blue beads and red tassles hanging round its neck. When they heard his voice far off, the women would snatch up their clashing tin buckets and come running, their headscarves streaming behind them. As they ran, Ali would start crying, 'The water of Harip won't swell the belly, the water of Harip won't burn your inside!' Then as he grew hoarse from shouting, the women would bang their tin buckets together and begin singing 'Harip gives water as good as our well!' Then Ali would lean back, swaying his shoulders until they touched the donkey's rump. He would kick out his feet in a dance and wind the red tassles round the blue beads. Having finished his water-selling dance, he would disappear shouting from among the huts. When he was out of sight he talked to the donkey.

As Ali talked to the donkey, one by one the blue beads fell on the roads between the huts, and the red tassles blew away in the wind. It was the installation of the first water-pipes in the huts that drove the donkey away from the garbage hills. Ali gave up selling water and began to mind the pigs at night on the lower slopes of the garbage hills. A week later, his wife Veliman sat herself at the window, leaning her face on her hand. The brightness of a full moon gleamed on her face. One of the watchmen came and blew his whistle. 'Why not just once?' he whispered. Veliman cursed and swore at him for many nights but finally she grew weary of staying up for Ali and stopped swearing. 'All right', she said, 'for a price'. She struck a bargain with the watchman and led him to her bed. The watchman told others, and while Ali minded the pigs in the farmyard all the watchmen in the area left teeth marks on Veliman's neck. She soon made a reputation as 'watchmen's Veliman'. She beat up three women from the huts who spoke and giggled behind her back, then went into her hut in a fury. She bared her neck at the window for the wind to blow dry the beads of sweat and as she sat looking up at the sky to get her breath back, the wife of one of the watchmen came pounding at her door. Veliman snatched up the bread knife and slashed the woman's mouth and tore out her hair. In the end she left Bald Ali and disappeared. Then Ali gave up minding the pigs and started lamenting on the garbage hills. He shed as many tears as the canfuls of water he had once sold on those roads. While he went about crying, Mr. Izak set up a makeshift factory on the slopes across the garbage hills and the hut people heard that workers were being taken on at the refrigerator factory. Ali broke off his lament for Veliman and joined the refrigerator workers.

> *Hairless Ali, don't you cry!*
> *We'll have a laugh at your expense*
> *Without a bit of fun we'd die.*
> *So up you go and have a turn,*
> *Cold iron might improve your burn.*

M r. Izak's factory was put together in the same makeshift way as the squatters' huts. Hundreds of guesses were made about Mr. Izak's origins, where he was born and grew up, and where he had come from to the garbage hills, but not a trace of his roots was discovered. In the settlement Mr. Izak put down his name as belonging to no homeland; he was as humble as the streams that ran between the hills. He wore workers' overalls and poured sweat like the other workers. He applied all his strength to one thing only — his machinery. Those who saw him thought he had been delivered on the garbage dump.

When darkness settled pitchblack over the factory he went home; and in the mornings, before any of his thirty-seven workers, he climbed the garbage hills and opened the factory gate again. He worked until he ran out of breath. Very soon, as he installed machinery, tools and workers, and also made certain changes to the building to go along with the machinery inside, his factory no longer bore any resemblance to the huts. He had the top half of the windows painted grey so the workers could not look up from their work at the dazzling slopes of the rubbish mounds. He had an iron door attached to one side of his factory. The traces of tears on Bald Ali's face wrung his heart, and he quietly slipped into his pocket a present of a spare key to the iron door, advising him to hurry up in the mornings and open the door before the rest of the workers got there. After that he had a guard placed at the door and made him search the workers as they left. Every evening he took on ten more men who did not mind being searched.

As production improved, Mr. Izak relaxed his discipline at work. One day he would arrive before all the workers and another day later than Bald Ali. One of his late days he did not put on his overalls and when the workers were eating at midday break Master Gülbey the ironworker said, 'Izak has become the gaffer.' The men guffawed as they ate. Mr. Izak slipped amongst them and asked news of their sick wives and home towns. He took out his wallet and gave them pocket money for their children. From then on the overalls were discarded: only his speech was like the workers'. He said he shared his fate with the settlers and that he too would spend his life with his eyes burning from the refrigerator chemicals on the slopes of the garbage dump. He called them all 'Garbage Brothers'.

In the huts the hammering and plastering never let up. No sooner was one wall repaired than another collapsed, and then a roof leaked, and one day bits of tin would be nailed to hut walls and on another bits of wood were put up to cover the gaps. A particular saying grew up in the squatters' language — 'The hut fences walk when the moon rises but near the graveyard they stand still'. Thus they described the character of their huts held together with pieces of wire and wood.

Mr. Izak's factory was only too pleased to be so unlike the huts. Work was never-ending, and there was always building, banging and hammering going on. Like the hut boundaries which walked at night, the garden wall moved as the huts tumbled down but, unlike the huts, never stopped as it got near the graveyard. When Mr. Izak approached the graveyard he recited a short prayer, then went underground. As the fumes filled the huts from the refrigerator chemicals, he had narrow tunnels dug under the slopes opposite the garbage hills. Big and little cells were opened up and new underground sections of his factory were installed beside the dead. Rumours soon spread through the huts, which shook from the rumbling below, that Mr. Izak would waken the dead and set them to work and would suffocate the living with refrigerator chemicals and lay them in the graves of the dead. He inspired fear and anger by embellishing the garbage mounds with bones and hollow skulls for the hut children to play with. The belief grew that this would bring bad luck to the huts.

To clear his name of this superstition Mr. Izak sent word to the foremost hut people and held meeting after meeting with them in his factory. He declared he would distribute milk to those suffocating from the chemicals. He poured milk down their throats by the gallon; then he built them a mosque next to his factory. Their growing anger vanished like the foam on the milk he distributed, a litre a day, for the following year. But as Mr. Izak's reputation grew velvet and creamy, his iron fist began to show. Under the mosque he built a storage vault for the refrigerators, and tunnels to connect it to the factory. He opened up more new underground rooms and installed new workers in them. Besides refrigerators he started to turn out washing-machines, radios and cookers. To distinguish the workrooms from the graves he had fluorescent lighting fitted in the ceilings, and the following names were inscribed on the doors:

METALWORKS
GLAZING
PLASTICS
WELDING
POLISHING
LATHE WORKSHOP
ASSEMBLY SYSTEMS
PAINTWORKS

In time Bald Ali's spare key grew tarnished and rusty and he kept it as a memento of Mr. Izak. Working underground with the others he melted away, dried up and choked. He coined an expression and passed it round all the workers — 'We took over the garbage hills but were moonstruck and forgot what was underneath'. While the workers were laughing together and inventing sayings full of references to Mr. Izak's underground factory, Ali mimicked his voice at midday break and nightshift, and made speeches starting — 'Brother Workers!'. After every speech he pulled the key from his pocket and pretended to open the doors. The workers guffawed and shouted — 'Sign us a leave-of-absence chit, Bald Ali!', and he signed cigarette papers. In a voice pitched high against the roar of the machinery he told them stories of the days when Mr. Izak had worked alongside them. Half the stories were mangled in the press and half were stifled on the conveyor belt. As Ali forgot some of the stories from tiredness and began to sing and dance halfway through others, the workers on the assembly lines never took him seriously.

> *At the factory doors*
> *Four workers stood.*
> *Over the garbage hills*
> *Sleet fell in showers*

In the days of the young thugs whose gunfire had startled the snow-white seagulls into a flight covering the sky with a black cloud, big tough guys had swaggered about Rubbish Road. The workers knew them as the Bully Boys. Workers who talked about unions, or insurance, or compensation, were beaten up until the blood flowed, and their yells mingled with the roar of the machines.

Smoke went on pouring from the chimneys and in time the workers in the factories strung along Rubbish Road joined a union, and the Bully Boys became a legend. Now the machine roar mingled with shouts from the factory owners sitting down at their tables to collective bargaining.

> *'Child allowance? And what's that?'*
> *'They'll come to the factory at festival time.'*
> *'They'll kiss our hands.'*
> *'We'll give them pocket-money.'*

When the men of Rubbish Road made a move to enroll in the union, Mr. Izak took on a new factory manager. They heard that Mr. Izak's new man had come from another country far away and that his first job would be to have hostels built on two of the garbage hills for the factory employees. His name resounded through Rubbish Road like the great seas which surrounded the country he came from and where he had been educated.

The manager put his training into practice in the refrigerator factory. He summoned the workers and first congratulated them for being clever enough to use their neck cloths (issued to polish the refrigerators) for wiping away their sweat and making a mouth mask; then he announced that from now on they could not have the bonus they had had once a year. Instead he would give out biscuits and yoghurt on alternate days.

The workers turned as white as the yoghurt; the refrigerator fumes got into their wide-open eyes, their throats were hoarse and torn from coughing, and their breathing was strangled. The manager said he would install a ventilation system in the factory for those affected and added he was organizing a new method of paying their wages.

That day the workers heard that when a man came on to the new wage-rate, he would become a 'modern' worker and would be rated not by seniority but according to output, skill and job commitment.

A little later a new creature called 'The Regular Worker' appeared in the factory. Workers were divided into 'regulars' and 'irregulars', and the regulars were paid more by the hour. The irregulars winced every time they were paid and heard the word 'regular'; one of them rolled this word round his tongue and spat out the half that had passed into their slang as 'regs'.

> *Workers, faster, faster move*
> *Than the aeroplane above.*

> *What if my hand gets caught and trapped*

Before my foot can stop the press?
Your fingers will get crushed and torn,
A bloody mess!

Workers, faster, faster move
Than the aeroplane above.

Night and day, the 'Work Faster' song battered the ears of
the men in the refrigerator factory. It was introduced by
Mr. Izak's new manager who had learned it in the country
where he had been trained. The ten workers chosen as
regulars began to earn more by the hour than the others;
the regulars bent over their yoghurts, chatting and laughing, the others cursing and dawdling. Of the regulars, some
were more regular than others and were paid even more by
the hour. The more regulars finished their yoghurts fast
and got back to the conveyor belt. The lesser regulars who
earned less by the hour lined up after them. The irregulars,
their heads bent over their yoghurt bowls, looked up and
their eyes met. They began to talk. 'May the yoghurt stick
in the throat of the man who switched from a bonus to
yoghurt!', they muttered, and sitting down with their
spoons under their arms, refused to eat. The new manager
stood beside them, and in a voice soft as down invited them
to eat the yoghurt. The men laughed and spluttered over
their cream-covered bowls.

   That day the new manager tried to give four representa-
tives a kick down one of the roads which straggled and
disappeared between the huts below the garbage slopes.
But these four stood their ground and waited like four
refrigerators at the factory exit. The foreman who had
attacked the protesters with a screwdriver hid behind the
new manager as he addressed the workers assembled at the
conveyor belt:

'Dear workers of the refrigerator plant, will the union build you hostels on the garbage hills, with windows flaming bright from the garbage glitter? Will it install ventilation in the factory and make the chemicals evaporate in the blue sky?'

After the new manager had spoken he distributed forms and called on the men to resign from the union and sign the papers. The regulars rushed to sign, but the others looked at him askance, sharp as needles. He said he had come with a fever straight from his sickbed to the factory and asked them to hurry. 'Don't upset me, boys!' he said. They laughed at the new manager and his 'fever'. Master Gülbey detached himself from their jeer and squatted down by the metal plates; he took a hammer and hammered away at the distorted metal until he had straightened it all out.

Gülbey was a craftsman who had gone round the huts at night with union papers and had introduced the union to the factory. Everyone in Rubbish Road knew that Mr. Izak had pushed a case full of money at him to stop him; and there was delighted discussion in the factories of how Master Gülbey had untied the bundles of notes and scattered them like confetti among the men who waited quietly by their machines. Besides the confetti business he had also invented a one-man resistance show called 'The Plastic Works Sit-in', which went down in the history of their union and later spread to other factories on Rubbish Road. While Bully Boys still frequented Rubbish Road, Gülbey was caught with union cards on his person, for in those days he worked at a plastics press and was very keen on the union. Mr. Izak removed him and gave him no compensation. Master Gülbey refused to be parted from the machinery he had polished with his sweat and worn smooth by his breath over the years. When he was laid off he chained himself by the arms to his machine. This led to an uproar in the factory. He lay there pitifully curled up and declared he would stay there until the officials came from the Employment Office. Not a single man did any work in the factory until the officials were able to pinpoint the machine where Master Gülbey sat hung with chains and locks. The work shifts piled up. Night fell.

> His eyes are welding flames,
> His lashes iron rods.
> Gülbey the Smith,
> Gülbey

Now the men followed Gülbey back to their machines, pressed the pedals and grasped the hammers and handles of the welding machines. They seized linchpins and screws. The conveyor which moved from one worker to the next slowly began to turn. Nothing could be heard but the hiss of the welding, the hammering of the metal workers and the rumble of machinery. Now and then one of the men broke off and, climbing on to the storage depot, looked out for the four men planted outside.

Work went on with quiet urgency for two days in the fridge factory. On the third day production slowed down and, as the hammers softly caressed the metal discs, showers of sleet began to fall on the garbage hills. The flakes slid down the grey-painted windows until evening and the lights came on. The welding flames died down, machines were silent, the arms of the presses fell by their sides. The metalworkers rose up and threw down their hammers and one rushed forward to turn off the main switch. The men for the night shift filled up inside the factory in a rush. The welders with their tools rushed to the doors and windows which they bolted and welded, then a barrel was rolled into the middle. Taci Baba leapt up on the barrel. With eyes like huge plastic moulds, he shouted 'Metal workers! Lathe workers!' The veins on his neck swelled like cords; 'May our resistance be successful,' he said, calming his pounding heart with his right hand. He was roundly applauded and the men's hands were stretched out to one another as though celebrating a festival. The headmen and foremen sneaked away quietly from the 'hand-in-hand' game and disappeared in the dark corridors. The 'regulars', confused and subdued in a corner watched the workers embracing. The lesser regulars watched longer, and while the more regulars grew more frightened, the makeshift mosques on the garbage slopes gave the call to prayer.

It was the month of Ramazan and 'what's more', to use Bald Ali's phrase, all the workers, regulars and irregulars, were fasting. At Mr. Izak's unearthly yells they all broke their fast at the machines. While the gleaming sleet fell and vanished in the dark, trucks surrounded the factory and took over the garbage hills. Panic-stricken men, summoned from outside to vacate the factory, burned with the desire to escape and their eyes slid in fear to the dark corridors, the doors and windows.

Master Gülbey got the men together and squatted down. He declared he would bury anyone in the garbage mounds who tried to escape. The workers were trembling at Mr. Izak's shouts and yells; Gülbey stopped up their nostrils flaring with fear. He climbed up on the roof of the storage depot, jumped on one of the runaway workers and knocked him down — the sleet washed away the blood which spouted from the runaway's nose over the concrete.

Dense darkness settled on Mr. Izak's factory; for a moment he imagined that his factory would slowly melt and vanish in the darkness and by morning would have disappeared. 'Save my factory' he shouted. The sleet stopped falling. Inside, the men were in Master Gülbey's hands; outside, the trucks were on the alert. Once again the deep darkness was split by a harsh voice summoning the men outside. Gülbey leant on the window and looked into the night torn to shreds by Mr. Izak. He inhaled and gulped a mouthful of cigarette smoke and darkness, then brought the workers together and sat at the conveyor belt. 'We'll melt all the plastic and make imitation grenades', he said. His voice exploded in their ears and they were filled with terror from head to toe. Master Gülbey peered into his friends' shadowy faces. 'We'll make a fool of them, mates!' he said. He sent three men in place of the plastics workers who were keeping watch. The plastics workers melted down the material and made ten white balls, but the melted plastic stuck fast to the flesh of their hands and cold metal was pressed on the burns. 'We'll bounce a grenade on your heads', they cried in reply to the yells from the darkness.

The balls changed the workers' fear to hope: but neither fear nor hope lasted long in the sleety dawn down by the machines. The state of the workers suited the words Bald Ali had poured into their ears; those who had taken over the top of the garbage hills had once more forgotten what was underneath. They had thought it was as easy as taking a spoon out of yoghurt to sit by Mr. Izak's machines and do no work. In the night the three men sent to keep watch slipped away. The workers were angry that they had deserted, handing over their duty to the wind howling over the factory. But their curses soon gave way to fear: 'where will all this lead to?'

Taci Baba turned round and gave the huts a long long look. As if in reply darkness swiftly abandoned them and dawn appeared. Taci Baba's face lit up with the glitter reflecting from the garbage mounds, and he turned to the workers. 'We've not sized up this business properly,' he said, and he revealed the idea which illumined his face. Taci Baba's suggestion to gather the women and girls and get them to shout and yell in front of the factory caught on among the workers. Grey Hamit was elected to round them up from the huts and instructed to shout at the top of his voice by the garbage mounds, to lie down like a corpse and pretend to weep and wail if the women ignored him. He was sent off in haste and hope.

When Hamit took his grey head off to the garbage mounds the hut children were already up and spread along the mounds, and the hut people had gathered on their roofs. They echoed his shouts in unison. He wore a blue apron which he took off and waved like a flag to the huts, shrieking like an alarm bell — 'Women and girls!' 'They'll slaughter us! They'll murder us!' he yelled between the huts and threw himself about. He beat his grey head on the stones and peered mournfully at the women whose eyes were wide with curiosity. Grabbing their skirts with one hand and pointing to the factory with the other, he rounded up all the women, girls and children from the huts and followed the workers' instructions to the letter. While his ears rang with the women's shouts he moved into his act of weeping and wailing and, as he scooped up a handful of earth, simulated moans and cries burst from his throat. During the act the earth he had scooped up suddenly became a stone which stuck in his throat. Hamit turned his head painfully towards the women and swallowed, and as he looked at the flowery headscarves everywhere his eyes filled, he slowly drooped his grey head by the women's feet and began to cry.

The tears pouring from Grey Hamit's eyes became a torrent which swept the women to the factory door. As they were carried away crying and shouting, Hamit wiped his eyes on the blue flag he held. He stood up in triumph and asked for Granny Dursune's hut: he had heard of her in the factories in the days of the hut wreckers. He began to run down the stream. Granny Dursune looked at Grey Hamit's face smeared with earth and at his blue apron but she could not recognize the man diving breathlessly into her hut. 'It must be one of us, but which one?' she muttered. When she had listened to him she stuck a pistol into the waist band of her baggy trousers and marched from her hut.

Where Granny Dursune had sat herself down during the protest days, with the pistol in her baggy trousers, Mr. Izak later covered the spot with asphalt, drowning the screams from the women and girls of the hut community in tar, and opening the two main doors of his factory onto this square. The workers paced out the ground and found the spot where Granny Dursune had pulled the gun on Mr. Izak, and this became the meeting place of the fridge workers greeting each other at night-shift. When the workers were released from the underground machines and staggered to the surface, they raised their arms and breathed in deeply as they met the men on night-shift duty. With narrowed eyes and anxious hearts, the night-shift workers closely watched the men appearing from the doors which opened into darkness. 'More power to your lungs!' they murmured. They touched one another on the shoulder as they separated and the fresh air tore at the lungs of the emerging workers. Daylight pierced their pupils like a needle and their tired arms shielded eyes blinking with pain. The watchmen halted the men shading their eyes.

Have you taken, have you stolen
Mr. Izak's wires and bolts?
That is banned.
Bring your arm down, show your hand.

Mr. Izak's watchmen, recruited from the hut people, searched the workers while they were still dizzy and aching, but would find nothing but traces of work on their clothes, hands and armpits. Spots of white paint from the job had dropped like white feathers on the painters' shoes while they were at work. They had stuck cloth caps on their heads so their hair would not turn white in a single day and had the idea of making sweatcloths out of the refrigerator polishing rags which they hung around their necks and held to their mouths as masks while they worked. At the start of the factory dinner break, workers in the deeper sections who had to pass through pitch-black corridors would wait for the painters to come out first so as not to miss the canteen door. The corridors would turn white from the drops scattered by the painters from their faces, hands and caps.

Painters, white doves.

The polishers would drop their sandpaper and straighten up holding their tired aching backs. Their eyes met a pitch darkness as black as the metal dust sticking to their faces, and they lost their way even in the white-painted corridors. Their black faces merged with the dark and disappeared. To get rid of the oily black they used to wash before coming up to the surface, then rushed from the hot water desperate to clear their stifled lungs and blow out the metal dust lodged in their throats as soon as they could. 'The man in a hurry is streaked with black', they said. A black streak as thick as an eyebrow would remain somewhere on their faces. They would go home shivering, their hair wet-combed and traces of work on their noses and foreheads.

Polishers with black-streaked foreheads.

The metal workers laughed the loudest at these marks left in haste. As they laughed they used to bang their files on the hammers and cup their hands round their mouths and the rust from their hands would smear their lips and faces.

Metalworker giants, big-mouthed with rust.

The giant workers were pale but fiery-eyed, and their hearts were wrought of iron. Their workshop was down in the depths of the factory. Iron filings and rust rained on their lashes and filled their eyes, their pupils dry as dust. Even as they jeered at the polishers a cold anger lingered in their eyes. While they worked their ears were deaf to each other so they threw away their hammers and shouted in unison. Their shouts travelled up to the surface of Rubbish Road, and the factory workers there believed these shouts would cast a magic spell. Whenever the garbage hills echoed with the metalworkers' cries, all the fridge workers would come up to the surface and pitch a tent at the factory gate. They wrote all over the doors and windows and hung the tarry square with inscribed banners waving as the wind blew.

Whenever the fridge workers appeared at the surface the men from the Rubbish Road factories would hastily report that the lathemen did not want to join the strike and that the metalworkers had beaten them up with their iron rods and thrown them out. Every factory added a new angle to the tale and different stories accumulated. The hut community heard that someone had written on the door of Mr. Izak's ironworks, 'No metalworks — no rights'. Before they could make sense of this, news spread on Rubbish Road and the garbage hills that the lathemen wanted to pitch a mosque tent beside the strike tent. This got mixed up with the story of Mr. Izak's house with its indoor pool and his wife's youth and beauty. But no one talked about his wife's beauty once it was overshadowed by a rumour that underground Mr. Izak was making parts for firearms. The hut people eyed the fridge factory with hundreds of questions in their heads.

The era of the squatter factories on the garbage hills ended with these hundreds of unspoken questions. The workers' songs mingled with the hodja's voice — from the mosque built by Mr. Izak — as he preached that a strike meant pitching a tent against God. All these sounds got lost in the screechings of the seagulls, the noise of the refuse drums, and the hum of the community. The garbage hills never stayed still and after every protest the trucks dumped the city's rubbish a little further from the huts. The huts multiplied as they tried to keep up with the trucks and every night their fences moved nearer to the new garbage heaps. After witnessing the founding of Flower Hill, Mr. Izak suddenly disappeared. He had signed his name clearly in chemicals on the skies above the garbage hills, and he left the direction of his factory to the managers and to the day and night foremen. The garbage hills saw him no more.

> *The man who wrecked the huts has gone*
> *The man who woke the dead has fled*
> *To distant lands and homes with pools.*
> *He feared the garbage birds.*
> *Fridge-gas has stung him till he cries,*
> *He runs away with streaming eyes.*
> *The fridges go by lorryload*
> *The workers had to tramp the road.*

Mr. Izak's departure was like Kurd Cemal's. His physical body disappeared from the garbage hills but his name remained, inscribed in their heavens. After Kurd Cemal joined the Town Council they heard he was to set up another big factory which would turn out industrial refrigerators on Panty Way. And after a time his factory materialised.

Like a gleaming star above the garbage hills the inscription read:

> *'In a squatters' community*
> *the coffeehouse, hotel and prostitute*
> *come first everytime'*
> *Kurd Cemal,*
> *Member of the Municipal Council*

When the refrigerator factory got going on Panty Way the rumour spread that anyone on Flower Hill who had registered in Kurd Cemal's party would find work in the plant. The Flower Hill people all registered with Kurd Cemal, and the men gathered humbly at the top of the garbage hills or in front of the town hall to get recommendation cards from Kurd Cemal or Garbage Owner. But ten youths — the cream of Flower Hill — went to work for Mr. Izak and the rest had their names struck off Kurd Cemal's party register.

This event which resulted in an angry comment from the Flower Hill folk, 'We're free to sign up, free to drop out!' seriously undermined Garbage Chief's position in Flower Hill. At the time of the founding of the workers' settlement, a rift had opened between Garbage Chief and the hut people, on account of the money he grabbed and his leanings towards 'bureaucracy', but when he tried to close the gap by worming his way into their confidence, then rushing them into joining Kurd Cemal's party, their respect for him sank to zero. They started a rumour about prostrating themselves in front of Kurd Cemal in prayer five times a day, and the intensity of their swearing took Garbage Chief's breath away. His only solution was to outshine the star of Kurd Cemal's inscription that gleamed over the garbage hills. He took a deep breath and declared that Flower Hill must have a school. The hut people paid little attention, thinking the school idea would turn out to be a lie, like the brass taps and the electric cables that were to coil round the huts, but Garbage Chief kept his promise to take part personally in building the school and to bring out a photograph of Flower Hill in the newspaper.

As soon as they heard that the photograph of Flower Hill would appear, they looked on him again with favour. On his advice they hastily knocked up wooden moulds, and a breezeblock yard was set up in their midst. Garbage Chief poured the first mortar into the moulds, letting the sweat drip from his nose, and had his picture taken with the men in the yard. The photograph showed rejoicing and smiles on the faces of the women and children.

After the Flower Hill folk had their picture printed in the paper a long rectangular schoolhouse was built for them with two walls of breezeblock and a tin roof. Garbage Chief's heart, which had sunk to the ground, took off from the roof and flew higher than the stars.

Much later a young teacher came to the long low school dressed in a navy-blue suit and a collar and tie. He assembled the hut people in front of the schoolhouse and made a long emotional speech which began, 'As I said in one of my poems . . .' From then on he always drew examples from his poems when he spoke to the hut people, including his pupils. The Flower Hill folk called this young man the 'Poet Teacher'. He was fascinated by the darkening sky as the garbage birds spread their white wings to heaven and soon he acquired the habit of standing alone on top of the garbage hills. He astonished the hut people when he declared he could not get enough of the sight of the garbage hills under the evening sun, and that they filled a man's heart with melancholy. He wrote innumerable poems on the stifling odour, on the garbage glitter and the smoke that rose over Rubbish Road. He recited them to the hut people who turned incredulous eyes on the smoke and the garbage mounds. He collected the songs and games of Flower Hill, and started a folk-dance group of little girls from the huts.

The group went from door to door collecting the caps worn by boys on their circumcision. The Poet Teacher stuck them on his girl pupils' heads, turning the sequin letters of 'May God preserve him' to the back, and covering them with spangled muslin. He got his boy pupils to learn his poems by heart. The son of the squatter family who played for the hut people at weddings became the group's folk singer on the garbage hills. On Poet Teacher's invitation the hut people assembled at the school and there he opened the children's performance with a poetic speech beginning with a reference to the garbage stink that settled even on Flower Hill's bread. Then he moved on to the good days to come. The musician's son leapt forward holding a huge tambourine. As the girls spun round he began to sing 'Lorke Lorke, drinking ayran swelled her belly'. He made the squatters laugh as he sat down with knees crossed just like his musician father. Some of them got on their feet intending to line up opposite the tambourine and dance, but Garbage Chief and the elders of Flower Hill insisted that they should sit down again. The musician's son nearly passed out playing his tambourine before the squatters. Sweat sprang to his forehead and dripped down his cheeks. Then it was the children's turn to recite poetry. Poet Teacher took one of the children and made him stand on a wooden chair. The child looked at the crowd with huge wide-open eyes, his face ashen pale with excitement, then words spilled from his mouth about the winged darkness of the garbage gulls; 'Bird, bird, whose wing is night'. Halfway through the poem he stopped and swallowed, then raising his head helplessly to the flying birds he began to cry. His head dropped like the tears pouring from his eyes, and he couldn't look at the people any more from shame. Jumping off the chair with his head down, and peeping at the crowd fearfully from behind his curtain of tears, he saw first Garbage Chief weeping, then the elders of Flower Hill, followed by all the squatters. He was rooted to the spot by the gleaming teardrops.

While there was no end to Poet Teacher's poems about the garbage hills and the hut people, sham factories began to be built on Flower Hill. Poet Teacher, pencil in hand, stood and looked at the men running up factories on the garbage slopes. Strange feelings disturbed him, and his head reeled with a confusion of words. Under his lashes his eyes heavy and helpless flickered over the old factories surrounding the huts and the apartment blocks far far away. Then he took a piece of paper from his pocket and wrote on it, 'The garbage hills were washed in fake detergent'. He laughed at his line, then folded the paper and put it back in his pocket, wondering how to solve the mystery of the garbage hills and capture it in his poem.

As Poet Teacher clutched his pen tight, some of the scavenger women and girls went to work in the sham factories with the men. From morning to night, in these factories which had been set up in just a few days, they produced fake detergents, multi-coloured fruit powders and juices, mouth-scorching chocolates, liquid whiteners that would not bleach and soaps that would not lather. The girls poured liquids into bottles and powders into packets and the men burned their hands as they worked at the plastic presses. The artificial fruit powders and mouth-scorching chocolates spread from Flower Hill to other neighbour-hoods. In all the huts the washing was done with detergents that would not foam, and in all the huts the children cried for the blue and black fruit powders.

The hut people entertained visitors with these powders and stored up packet after packet for their most important guests. The powders turned into the juice of unknown fruits. The sham factories went on spreading, reaching from the huts right down to the Rivermouth Neighbourhood. And in time the site was given the name of 'Flower Hill Industries'. Small textile workshops opened on the site, and from them blue, green and red smoke blew into the sky. Clouds of all shapes and colours lay over Flower Hill. Factory snow fell on the huts and the clouds descended as coloured rain.

The factory snow melted in the coloured rains and all the names inscribed in deep black letters on the Flower Hill huts were washed away. Time passed and these sham hut-sized factories determined Flower Hill's destiny until other hut-factories were conjured up to circumvent the strikes. Flower Hill Industries produced new songs and customs for the hut people, but although a period of plenty arrived, their wounds did not heal. Flower Hill became a single hut with the sky as ceiling and factories as walls. Noise drowned noise.

Flower Hill Industries drew the squatters away from the garbage hills which were then abandoned to Poet Teacher and the gulls. Poet Teacher wrote a long poem comparing the scavenger birds to his pupils. One evening when his heart was heavy and he wanted to read his poem to the birds he muttered it with downcast head and dragging footsteps. But the birds fluttered their wings indifferently at Poet Teacher; for them there was only one poem possible about the garbage hills. The hut people had written it long ago. It was not very long. It was quite brief and consisted of one line recited through screams, shouts and stone throwing.

'Away with garbage!'

When garbage ceased to be a source of profit, rumours spread that the garbage flies would consume the squatters who would then breathe fire and flame at Garbage Owner and disown the garbage mounds. This, 'Away with garbage', which summed up the lives and experience of the squatters on the garbage hills, would be seen as the signal for action. The protest would be sparked off first by the gulls beating their wings and waking the sleeping babies, then flying skywards as they played the game of turning day into night. The birds would be stoned.

As a result of this state of affairs on the garbage hills, Poet Teacher's poem to the birds remained unfinished. A screech-fight broke out between the gulls and the squatters. Bruised and sore, the birds dropped their feathers over the garbage trucks and flew off into the clouds. Poet Teacher, bird feathers on his shoulders, gazed into the dark clouds which the squatters called, 'Bird cloud' and withdrew from the garbage mounds. After the birds the truck drivers who transported garbage to the slopes were attacked under the screeching clouds.

It was common knowledge how long this protest would last. Whenever the truck drivers came to unload garbage the squatters would drag them from their vehicles, beat them up and put them to flight before they could empty their trucks. Every time a new settlement sprang up they played this game of tit-for-tat.

But this time the game was joined by Garbage Owner, the garbage watchmen and the hut women who tore the fronts of their dresses and lay down before the trucks. As the quarrel and debate dragged on over which particular hilltop they would inundate with the truck drivers' blood, the gypsies' takeover of the garbage hills disrupted the usual course of their protest.

Although there was already a communal gypsy settlement among the hut quarters on the garbage hills, the Flower Hill people, busy with the garbage protest, assumed that the gypsies were merely migrants drawing breath as they passed through Flower Hill. But when the squatters had finished talking with them they knew that the gypsies had fallen in love with the magical coloured clouds rising to the heavens and would set up their own home on the garbage mounds along with a troupe of bears. Moreover, the gypsies would heal the wounds of the garbage gulls and search the garbage along with them for cardboard boxes to build houses to live in. Realizing this the squatters lost the urge to spill the truck drivers' blood on the garbage hills and took a break from protesting. A discussion arose as to the origins of the gypsies and so Honking Alhas, expert in gypsy lore, was rescued from oblivion among the huts.

Honking Alhas' livelihood resulted from his skill in erecting huts within the hour for inhabitants of other hilltops of the city. At the beginning of discussions he stood out for his wide knowledge of the gypsies who occupied the top of the garbage mounds, and of many more races as well. He declared the gypsies were people without a homeland or religion and, moreover, they were barbarians and on their identity cards was written 'Romany'. He said 'Romany' meant a person of uncertain origin. He gave the hut people a further piece of knowledge — that the gypsies were descended from a mountain very far away, half hidden in the sky, its height unknown, and they had dispersed all over the world hundreds of years ago. The names of the countries they had gone to were all recorded in Honking Alhas' mind. Quick as lightning he flashed out these names which the hut people were hearing for the first time and were quite unable to get their tongues round.

This flood of names which poured out in his honking pronunciation caused by a nasal obstruction, was inscribed in history, but the number of people in the world, let alone on the garbage hills, who knew these names now could be counted on one hand. To be able to imagine what it was like when the Romanies first settled in these parts, the squatters had to know about a certain 'Ottoman Empire'. So Honking Alhas left aside the Romanies for a while, feeling he had to tell the squatters that where they now lived there had once been an empire of this name. The squatters wanted detailed and accurate information on the gypsies, but he filled their ears with accounts of sultans, imperial edicts, cities with streets inlaid with wood, and golden doorknockers. And when he had confounded them with all that history had written about the Ottoman

Empire, he returned once more to the subject of the gypsies and pinpointed their most important characteristic. He said the gypsies were filthy and he blessed the sultan for issuing an edict to throw them out of the city whose inlaid streets they had defiled. He sighed as he told how, after the edict, the Romanies fled to the springs and reservoirs which supplied the city. They had passed into history as people who had polluted the water of this beautiful city where they lived. From his knowledge of history he affirmed that they would pollute Flower Hill and reduce it to an uninhabitable state. When he had described how the sultan chased them from the reservoirs and drove them out of the city and declared war on them, Alhas put his history back on the shelf. Gypsy women were very fat while the men were very slight, he said, and asked the hut people if they knew why this was so. They watched his mouth expectantly and laughed loud and long. Honking Alhas, nose in the air, answered his own question. He said the men swallowed pills which dissolved bones and shrivelled flesh and that they passed day and night in sleep and dreams. Every day their womenfolk plucked three hens each and ate them; this was why the gypsy women and girls were called 'Gacos' or 'birds'.

Honking Alhas' information about the gypsies roused such repercussions on Flower Hill that for days on end the main subject of inquiry was how the Gacos managed to find three hens a day to eat. All the other communities on the garbage hills heard about the pills that wafted people from dream to dream, and the stories of the three hens and the 'clove' of hashish — as Alhas used to call it. New information from the squatters who lived next to the gypsies mingled with Honking Alhas' accounts. And in this way the Flower Hill folk learned about the gypsy weddings, their ways of quarrelling and swearing, their fondness for music and their versatility in a thousand and one ways. But Honking Alhas thought the Flower Hill folk still did not know enough about the gypsies and he re-opened the dusty pages of history. He told them how the Romanies had been chased from the city by the sultan, had rebelled against the Ottoman Empire and after a lengthy struggle had set up camp and brought a great city of tents into being. Honking Alhas rolled the name of this city round his tongue for days and when he repeated again and again that there was nowhere else in the world like it, they thought on Flower Hill that his knowledge was exhausted. But Alhas proved he knew more about the gypsies than anyone else on the garbage hills when he spoke of their inroads on this country in 1936, long after they had founded their city. After his account of this and certain other events, the Flower Hill people understood that no one could compete with Alhas on the history of the world and humanity. Long before anyone had heard of the words 'hut' and 'garbage', a situation had developed in one of the great countries of the world. It was known as the 'Revolution', but seemed to mean a human whirlwind. Herds of Romanies were living in this country, wandering about playing their music. After the human whirlwind had come to rest, the name of this country was recorded in history as 'Communist' and in the new order which came about an old and splendid name was darkened. As the gypsies were barbarians who did not conform to order, the name 'Romany' was erased from their identity papers and replaced by 'Turk'. Thus in 1936 these non-conformers were trapped in their hordes among the Turks.

Alhas' astounding depth of knowledge made the hut people forget about the arrival of the gypsies on Flower Hill. His narrative was so embellished with references to unknown places and lists of dates that the squatters became curious about how all this knowledge had filtered into his head; they were no longer interested in the cardboard houses the gypsies would build or the pills that would float them to dreamland. Honking Alhas became the most talked-about squatter on the garbage hills. His hut was singled out from the others and people kept going up his street to knock on his door.

Throwing back his head haughtily and narrowing his eyes Alhas answered the questions put to him. He listed his reasons for accumulating all this knowledge, saying that the subject he had been most curious about all his life was the origin of human beings. The squatters gaped with amazement as he explained how he had discovered the chief ancestors and greatest saints of all the races of men. He told them the story of some of the races. He announced that the Laz were the grandchildren of the fishing tribes who had come as settlers from the north seas and that their ancestor was Chief Istafanos, leader of the first tribe to arrive. He smiled as he reminded them that most of the Laz did not even know the name of their ancestor. After Chief Istafanos he named a holy man of the Chinese, 'Konfektyon', and had much to say about him. He told them that the people of China lived their lives according to his teachings which they kept in a huge book that was one of the most valuable in the world. Then he gave them some of Konfektyon's counsels.

Konfektyon's name and counsels brought fame to Honking Alhas almost as great as Mr. Izak's and Kurd Cemal's. He felt he had to have a suit of shiny sky-blue material tailor-made for himself to merit the interest shown by the squatters. First he welcomed the squatters who came to his hut to receive Konfektyon's words of wisdom and learn the names of their ancestors, then he withdrew to his back room. Donning his shiny sky-blue suit he came out to meet them. His hair was combed back except for a single wet curl, shaped like a rose leaf, which fell on his forehead. He raised his head high and took his place on the divan to deliver his lessons in history and humanity.

As the Flower Hill folk sat gazing at Honking Alhas on his divan, innumerable cardboard houses were set up on the garbage mounds. The gulls had their legs bandaged and came back to life, and while they perched on the backs of the bears and flew back and forth, the cardboard houses were having their interiors decorated with an assortment of objects retrieved from the garbage. Lines were stretched from one corner to another, and plastic dolls scavenged from the garbage, their hair and arms torn off, hung from them like bunches of grapes. Old fashion magazines thrown on the refuse heaps were stuck up on the cardboard walls, pinned open at their cover pages. The rest of the spaces were adorned with coloured glossy paper picked from the rubbish and cleaned up. Round or flattish bottles and tin cans with picture labels hung from the ceilings. Volumes of books in languages which even the Romanies did not understand were rescued from the garbage and spread on the floors. The divans made of garbage books were covered with gull feathers. The centre pages of the fashion magazines dangling on the walls like lanterns, turned this way and that to the sound of bağlama and tambourines. The shiny coloured paper gleamed, and feathers flew about in the cardboard houses. The voices of Romany children and the sounds of Romany instruments streamed into the huts of Flower Hill and some of the squatters went to see, wondering what it was like in the decorated homes of the Romanies. They described what they saw and others in turn reported what they heard. The cardboard décor of the garbage mounds and the gypsy songs which ran, 'the moon turns with a rustle, the huts gleam', spread to the huts of Flower Hill.

Under paper sheets
Romanies shiver.

The moon rustled and turned. The factories gleamed, and the men worked faster than flying. The moon sank, the sun came up, and over the garbage hills the shouts of the metal workers rose to the heavens. In the huts vibrating with these cries they heard that the metal workers from the refrigerator factory were being joined by other workers on their march to Minibus Way. It was reported that the marchers were homeless men without families who would try to attack the people and take away their homes. Further rumours followed that the marchers on their way had smashed the factory windows and beaten up laggard workers, forcing them to join the march. Then the hut community rose up to follow the workers. Rubbish Road, only just cleared of the marching, shouting workers who waved banners overhead, now filled up with squatters pouring from the huts and cardboard houses. Flower Hill was empty except for a few people fearfully nailing boards over their doors and windows and securing them with locks. While they kept guard on their huts, the sound of distant gunfire halted the squatters as they followed behind the workers. News rippled through the crowd that the workers were clashing with the police, at which point the crowd began to flow back, colliding with the huts, and broke up in Flower Hill's narrow alleys.

On Minibus Way the workers' banners were torn to shreds and their cudgels broken. The sun seemed to rustle and turn. On Asphalt Road a worker was shot and died shouting along with the others, 'If you grab the worker's share, it'll stick in your throat.' The sun withdrew and sank behind the rubbish mounds.

The wingbeats of the gulls tore the smoke from the Flower Hill Industries to rags; dispersing slowly, it mingled with the dappled sky. The gleam of the garbage hills died away. In the cardboard houses the gypsies left off playing and singing, and while a rumour swept through the huts like a gust of wind that the workers' unions would be closed down, mother-of-pearl buttons opened over Flower Hill. The stars shone. Bejewelled with huts, the world's face darkened, and night fell. Those who complained they had had enough of the workers and their pigeons, tents and unions went to bed early and slept. But others who were shocked and bewildered by the workers' march assembled in the huts.

From his knowledge of the world and human nature, Honking Alhas was the first to maintain that communism had come to the garbage mounds and that the community's unity and harmony would be destroyed. From now on, he declared, they would have no sleep. He reminded them of the days when Garbage Owner had sent large tins of halva to the fridge workers' strike tents and claimed that the workers would never again taste halva from Garbage Owner. The word 'halva' became a joke to the simit-sellers on Rubbish Road and the silent seagulls on the cardboard houses. Bayram of the Pine (the only one on Flower Hill to have a pointed pine tree before his hut) said that what had come to Flower Hill was not communism but workers from the bicycle and cable factory with star and crescent flags. He repeated what the workers from the seacoast had shouted when they met and mingled with the men from the garbage hills. Waving his hands about, he declared that most of them were guffawing as they marched and had no idea of what would happen. Mikail the simit-seller, well known among the workers on Rubbish Road for his mimicry of all kinds of animal cries and best of all for birdsong, backed up Bayram of the Pine. He described how the women in their white headgear streamed from the chemical factories like a foaming torrent, and swore it was a lie that the workers had beaten up the men unwilling to come out. He said they had marched in an orderly way, but when they saw the women thrown down and beaten they had flared up in anger. 'The women were treated very badly', he said, and he called his two eyes to witness, beady as a bird's. He said most of the women were screaming and shrieking from broken arms and backs. Never again would they be able to lie on their sides, he grieved, then opened his mouth and gave vent to screams like the screams of the women being dragged along the ground.

The hut people condemned the men who had encouraged the women to go into the street and get beaten up. They argued fiercely about male honour being represented by women, and they all agreed that at the next flare-up the men should not stand back and let the women go into the front line.

While angry shouts were being exchanged on this subject in the workers' settlement, Simit-seller Mikail began to do an impersonation of a worker on Flower Hill hit by a stone at the base of his neck. He clutched his neck and crashed to the ground at the hut people's feet. Their eyes were wide with excitement and as he looked at them, he yelled, 'Save me!' Then he got up and suddenly turned into a policeman. While he was running off he got caught among the wires over the road. Hands raised, he mimicked the policeman gasping with terror, and the hut people couldn't help laughing at his antics. He dropped his hands to his sides and said that if a general (which he pronounced 'gerenal') stopped a worker on the march and asked him where he was going, the worker would be nonplussed. Comparing the workers to quarrelsome colts, he swore they had no idea where they were going. What he said about the generals showed his real feelings. He summed it up in a simple phrase

> *Suppose the generals had met*
> *The men on Asphalt Road*

This final phrase of Simit-seller Mikail, who had looked on the torrent of workers with his eyes full of poetry, was the gem among the myriad words uttered on Flower Hill after the march. And whoever heard it laughed till they cried. While he was selling his simits and mimicking the birdsong on Rubbish Road, tears rolled down people's cheeks. As he watched he imagined his name shining high above Flower Hill. But he wasn't chosen from the hut people to become a star, for one morning before daybreak a fire broke out and burned the cardboard houses to ashes. The gem lay buried beneath.

One of the garbage tales, known as 'The Great Garbage Fire' was about Chief Mahmut, the head of the gypsies, and Crazy Dursun the squatter and the five gypsies who died by fire. It ran on and on in couplets that were rooted in the speech of the squatters who lived on the garbage hills.

> *From the rooftop Crazy Dursun had a view*
> *Of the gurgling kettle as it poured its brew.*

'The gurgling kettle' was the name the Flower Hill folk gave to Chief Mahmut's samovar which stood in the gypsy chief's cardboard residence. It was a magnificent creation, with its slender tubes dovetailed together and the big shining teapot with its strainer. Chief Mahmut would sit cross-legged by this samovar that gleamed like a mirror, while he crowned the hut people's rotten teeth. Everyone who entered the chief's cardboard house came out equipped with teeth gleaming like tinned copper and delighted with the gypsy tales dropping from Mahmut's lips. Chief Mahmut was not only expert at crowning teeth but also at filling the gaps with teeth as good as real. He re-silvered mirrors and re-tinned pots and pans. He had seven wives and twenty-one children. But the apple of his eye was his youngest wife Zülika whom he was said to have kidnapped. She was a Posha gypsy. Squatters who entered Chief Mahmut's cardboard abode were dazzled by Zülika and she became famous on Flower Hill. Her sparkling teeth bright as the full moon, her crescent eyebrows and long wavy hair that swung at her heels in a knot created the 'Posha legend' and the belief that the beauty of the Posha gypsies was fatal.

While Zülika was the sole subject of conversation devoured by the hut people, Crazy Dursun of Flower Hill left his mother's hut and settled by the gurgling kettle at Chief Mahmut's knee. He never stuck his head outside the house of cardboard. Crazy Dursun's migration from Flower Hill to the cardboard houses gave rise to a string of jokes. Then these subsided and rumours grew that Zülika had been seen going down Panty Way at the dead of night having fun with Crazy Dursun in the breezeblock yards. These rumours reached Chief Mahmut's ears while he was silvering a mirror by his gurgling kettle. But he just looked in the mirror and laughed, showing his gleaming teeth, his own handiwork.

Three years before he moved to the cardboard houses Crazy Dursun used to polish shoes on Rubbish Road. One midday as he was dozing off by his shoe box, his shaved head burned in the sun's rays and he got sunstroke. His brain seethed. The brush he held rolled out of his hand and he too fell to the ground. He began to thrash about; banging his head to right and left, he collapsed exhausted and fell asleep in the arms of two watchmen from the factory. For three years he never rose from his bed but lay breathing deeply, subjected to all kinds of attempts to cure him by the Flower Hill people. The illness, which befell him in his fourteenth year, eventually cleared up in his seventeenth but left him in a dazed condition. His chin which had slipped over to his left ear righted itself but his wandering wits never came back to their nest and kept rocking like a cradle inside his head. On account of the tumult in his head his eyebrows were set in a moody frown and he wore a peevish angry expression. During the day he would take his peevishness through the Flower Hill streets; at night he was inconsolable. He undid his shirt buttons in a fit of distress and punched himself repeatedly until he was panting and groaning, and when the Flower Hill people had gone to bed he rushed outside, then beat on their doors with all his strength. 'Hey, get up! I'm in a bad way!' he shouted and cursed the sleepers. If anyone opened the door he slipped in and sat in the best seat, breathing hard with anger. But the community had had enough of Crazy Dursun's night time visitations. In the alleys of Flower Hill his whole body would be seized with convulsions, and when the fit was over he would lie down motionless on the road to sleep off his exhaustion.

One night when he rushed out in one of his fits his attention was caught by the sounds of music. He discovered Chief Mahmut's headquarters on top of the garbage mounds, and from that night he left the squatters' doors in peace. But as he gazed and gazed into Zülika's dark eyes he was stricken for the second time. His heart burned with love, and Crazy Dursun began to fear Zülika with her burning dark eyes. He ran away from Chief Mahmut's house and climbed up to his mother's roof. And for days and nights on end he kept unbroken watch on the cardboard house where Zülika lived.

Towards the end of summer he saw policemen approaching the garbage mounds and he left his post. His ears were full of the grumblings of the gypsies' bears and the gulls beating their wings on the rooftops.

By the time Garbage Owner's white car had driven down Rubbish Road and disappeared from sight, all hell had broken loose before the cardboard houses as screams and shouts from the gypsies rose and fell. The gypsies banded behind Mahmut their chief, charged at the garbage, and the huge mound which stood beside the cardboard houses was hurled noisily in gleaming pieces in the direction of the huts. The noise of gunfire from the policemen as they aimed in the air was drowned in the rumble of the collapsing garbage.

After the policemen had scattered in the Flower Hill streets, a ditch was dug on the garbage slopes. A row of bears lumbered to the ditch and jumped in. And in a flash, cans, stones, bottles piled up at the back of the ditch. As the policemen made a move towards the gypsies, the stones and cans and bottles were thrown to the bears who hurled them all at the policemen. The hut people gathered on their rooftops to see how well the bears had been trained. But to Crazy Dursun the bears' endeavour seemed tragic; he knelt down crying, chin in hands. While the bears were brandishing stones with all their might, he jumped from the roof in tears, and crossing to the gypsies gathered stones to help the bears.

The hut people who had climbed up to their rooftops to watch, leapt down when the policemen left and rushed to the cardboard houses. Gypsies and hut people mingled together, but Crazy Dursun stole away from the uproar and went back to his post on his mother's roof. Once again he fixed his eyes on the cardboard houses and gazed at the garbage hills through a mist of tears. Silence settled on Flower Hill. Well after midnight the gypsies and the hut people fell into a deep sleep.

Three of Garbage Owner's men came to the garbage mounds and one crept up to a cardboard house and silently set it on fire. Flames leapt from house to house. The seagulls' feathers frizzled, the bears' hides were flayed off their backs and the stench of burned flesh and feathers enveloped Flower Hill as it awoke to the gypsies' shrieks.

Out in the street they saw the gypsies walking round and round the ashes which had been their homes and the birds circled overhead. Half asleep, they made for the garbage mounds where Chief Mahmut sat by the dead bears and gypsies, surrounded by the survivors. The hut people drew round them at a distance and watched in silence as the gypsies struck palm to palm and muttered in Romany. The dead bears and gypsies were buried up on the garbage mounds.

New cardboard homes were set up as the ashes of the dead blew through the Flower Hill streets. Tomato paste was smeared on the seagulls' burns; their wings turned red.

S now fell.

The Flower Hill people woke from their deep shivering sleep to the booming of the Ramazan drum. Behind the drumbeats lights sprang up, and the drummer walked the streets of Flower Hill turning darkness into a road of light. As he flourished his drumstick he opened his mouth and chanted some folk verse to the huts still buried in darkness . But just as he was about to beat his drum he heard a voice from the dark, 'Get the Hell out of here!' His stick remained poised in the air as a shower of oaths poured on his drum, his drumstick, his hand, his face and the noise he was making. It was impossible to pass beyond the barrier of oaths so he retreated in silence and in the early hours of the morning he beat on the ornate doors of the Flower Hill mosques with their tin minarets. Rallying a crowd of squatters behind him he made for the district he had just been chased from. In the cold snowy daylight they could hardly see one another but a slanging match broke out. The hut people got hold of the idea that the man who cursed the drummer was one of the Kızılbaş sect, and Flower Hill was soon agog with an ever-growing story about the Kızılbaş.

> *Daughter with father,*
> *Mother with son,*
> *All whirled about.*
> *When the dancing was over*
> *The candle went out.*

By noon the next day the ritual assemblies of the Kızılbaş, their Elders and disciples, their sacred tree and the gifts presented to the Elders, were no longer secret from the rest of the hut people. They discovered that the Kızılbaş of Flower Hill belonged to fifteen different fraternities. They learned by heart the name of each fraternity, called after its presiding Elder, and the birthplace of every Kızılbaş member. Once they had established where the disciples lived they moved on to scrutinize their sexual habits. Debate raged on how 'the candle went out' during the Kızılbaş rituals, while the sun withdrew, shedding a dim half-light as suggestive as the tone of their conversation.

By the time it grew dark, they had divided on the question of whether the Kızılbaş fasted or not. Those who claimed that they ate only raisins during Ramazan went back to their huts after the evening prayers, and the rest who had no such conviction about the Kızılbaş went the drummer's way, to gather all the musical instruments they could collect from the huts.

A band was formed from a bağlama, a tambourine, a banjo, a fiddle, a zurna and a drum. As though they were off to a wedding they headed straight for where the Kızılbaş lived, the squatter musicians in front and the trouble-makers in the rear. They played until daybreak, marching up and down in front of the doors of the Kızılbaş community. The man who had cursed the drummer panicked and boarded up his door and window. Demonstrating the famous Kizilbaş tolerance he lay sweating under five layers of quilt, taking refuge in daydreams. As he fell to dreaming the music stopped and a quarrel broke out between the squatters who had rushed indignantly out of doors, and those parading up and down the road. The quarrel grew with the speed of the light that was now illuminating the huts. Those hut people who had come from many different villages and settled down together now formed a united front. While the fight dragged on, the one and only coffeehouse which served the Flower Hill Industries fell into the hands of the Kızılbaş squatters, and that was how during the brief nights and long days they spent together in their huts the rest of the hut people gained deeper knowledge of the truth about the Kızılbaş of Flower Hill.

Only after a whole year, when the community had settled down, was Flower Hill ready for a visit from the Kızılbaş Elders. A long time ago the Elders had come to the city having heard that the Kızılbaş had huts there and were preparing wonderful ceremonies in their honour. Unaware that these Elders who circulated the huts begging for handouts of money and gifts had been turned away by the squatters, an Elder and his son set off from a distant city with the same idea and came to Flower Hill, claiming blood ties. He also brought along an impressive stick to beat the

Kızılbaş who did not observe their duties. His followers believed he was held high in God's esteem as he had eaten nothing but butter and cheese from the day he was born. But on Flower Hill his stick was of no use to him. No one took any notice even when the squatter in whose home the Elder was a guest spread the word that this Elder had long ago predicted men going to the moon and the invention of television. The squatter's hospitality to the Elder and his son went on for months, but when he realized that no one had any respect for them he finally turned them out. For a time they wandered about appearing at people's doors hoping for handouts. The Elder left his stick as a keepsake and withdrew to be with God, never to return. His son took up business, put aside his father's stick and began to sell fake blue jeans.

The other squatters had not the slightest change of heart when they heard about this sad turn of events. The quarrel which had gone on in secret broke out into occasional fisticuffs in the alleys. Gradually all their anger focussed on Flower Hill's single coffeehouse which the Kızılbaş had taken over as their property, swelled into fury at their own ineffectual raids on the coffeehouse, and eventually exploded. Fifteen coffeehuts sprang up in fifteen separate corners of Flower Hill in a single day, and rage and quarrels were replaced by gambling and coffeehouses. Gamblers from other squatter areas began to frequent Flower Hill and rumour had it that a famous gambler, nicknamed 'Lado' on the garbage slopes, would be moving to the hill.

Lado was the first hero to be created by the coffeehouses on the garbage hills. Long before the rumour that he was moving to Flower Hill, every night of his life had been eagerly worked up into a separate adventure and on Flower Hill, even when the number of coffeehouses on Nato Avenue alone had reached 150, Lado's adventures remained as the finest examples of the squatters' oral tradition. All his life Lado had sought an answer to the question, 'Who was greater, God or the man who invented gambling?' His special gear and garments, the time he stole from gambling to write the novel about his life, and his reasons for divorcing four wives, all played a part in making him a hero. Lado had won the right to be recognized as a remarkable gambler not just for his skill in gambling but for his colourful life.

White was one of Lado's colours

Summer and winter Lado wore sharp-pointed white shoes with platform heels which he never took off but preserved very carefully from the dusty muddy roads of the garbage hills. In his back pocket he carried a dark red velvet cloth to polish them up when they got dusty. On the strength of his first winnings from gambling he had two black satin waistcoats made with belted backs. A metal buckle shaped like a devil's head with sharp horns was fastened to his waistcoat belt. And round his neck he hung one of the devil heads on a solid shining chain. His fondness for lace and pink showed in his shirt. He embellished the upper half of his body with a dawn-pink shirt with cuffs made from three layers of ruffled lace. His jacket with its broad rounded lapels and flared trousers of black and white stripes were chosen in the best taste. The final touch was a white handkerchief in his jacket pocket, its corners displayed on his breast like an open rose. While echoes of his reputation ran through the coffeehouses he cleverly created a new image. He gave up the laugh that sounded like wooden logs thudding from a horse-drawn cart and put on a fixed smile fit for a hero. At every fountain he saw he got into the habit of washing his hands a long long time. Then with a shake of his shoulders he drew the white handkerchief from his pocket and dried his hands on it.

Lado — a butterfly with spangled wings

He had meant to live for many years with his first wife whose fragrance, he believed, came from the flowers of her native village. But one evening Lado's wife used a hot iron on the black nylon socks he wore inside his white shoes. Lado angrily grabbed the crumpled socks and dragged his wife outside. With tears in her eyes she tried to clutch his flared trousers, but Lado's ears were stopped with anger, and he was deaf to his wife's entreaties. Though later on he gave way to the insistence of the go-betweens and consented to make up with his wife, he was not willing to renew his marriage. He took the care of their children upon himself and gave her only friendship.

Ten days after separating from his first wife Lado began to lust after the sister of another gambler who was making a name for himself on the garbage mounds. Burning with this passion and unable to bear the agony, he got himself engaged. His fiancée made him an embroidered necktie covered with coloured sequins and beads, and Lado wore it with his pink shirt. For the wedding he took over the three biggest coffeehouses. After the wedding to which Kurd Cemal's men, together with the gamblers of the garbage hills, paid a visit and distributed largesse, Lado failed to appear in the coffeehouses for seven days. In the following nights his weary smile made everyone at the gaming tables envious. He leaned back stretching his legs to full length. But this wife gave Lado's dawn-pink shirt to the mice to eat. He did not forgive her carelessness, and affecting a nervous blink, divorced her too.

His two matrimonial disappointments made him take a third 'wife' without marrying her. The bride came quietly and was made known to Lado's closest friends in a very simple ceremony. Lado offered sweets to his friends while his wife sat shyly on the divan. As she was lame Lado forbade this wife to go out. For months she submitted to his orders but became depressed at being stuck between four walls and went to a wedding without telling Lado. Lado claimed that he had come home and found the pots and pans empty and had gone to bed hungry that night, so he took his third wife home to her father as quietly as he had brought her.

He went far afield in search of a fourth wife, found one and brought her from her own country. He agreed to pay a large price for his young bride who lacked three more years to be half his age. But soon after he decided to write his autobiography she became victim, according to Lado, to her own insensitivity and foolishness.

Once Lado became an inveterate gambler he fell for the exciting tales and rumours he had generated and got it into his head to make a novel out of his life-story. Till then he had read only a slim, yellow-paged book of Karacaoğlan's life and poems. So he went off to visit one of Kurd Cemal's men who worked in the municipal office, got one of his books and soaked himself in it. He started to record in a secret notebook the recollections which he had put in order in his head, but then lost heart during the exercise. News spread on the garbage hills, however, that Lado was going to write a novel. Too late he realized that he had subjected his carefully-clad body to a heavy responsibility. Everyone who heard that Lado was to write a novel knocked at his door, and the gamblers of the hut community competed to encourage him. Through a justifiable mistake the story of Lado's life was understood by the hut people to be the history of the garbage hills. Invitations began to pour in and in the houses he visited people placed cushions under his feet and at his back. He was moved by the quavering voices of the people as they vied with one another in telling the thousand and one sad tales of their experiences. He felt he owed something to the hut people when they said, 'Let's all make a nice novel together'. So he decided to write the story of his own life at least, if not of the garbage hills.

Every day he got up from his usual gambler's sleep two hours earlier and shut himself in his back room. Six months later he had managed to write the first half page of his novel. He made his gambler friends and other dilettantes in the coffeehouse read the half page he had written. Those who read it declared that Lado's novel would be one of the greatest ever written. He picked up speed when he saw the smiles on people's faces as they read his half page and he shut himself up confidently in his room and for a whole month forgot the way to the coffeehouses. On waking every day he grabbed his pencil and settled down with his paper. During that month he never took a comb to his greying hair; he never took off his pyjamas which got worn out at the knees, and he wandered around his house in a dream without looking at his wife and children. He was unaware of the rising anger in his wife's eyes. She finally lost her temper as he wandered about abstractedly in a totally different fantasy house. She stood in the way of his daydreams and planted herself before him with clenched fists. He was overcome by fury at her shrieks. Breathing rapidly he leapt on her and showed her what it meant to disturb the delicate balance of a mind hanging by a thread between dreams and reality. She lay on the floor like an empty sack which Lado left lying as he clung to the curtains and walls. He rushed out, leaving the children yelling with fear.

While Lado was nostalgically inhaling the air of the garbage hills his wife set fire to his writings. For Lado this was the last straw. He divorced her, but because of his pain and rage he could not take up a pen again and in order to forget, he gave himself up to gambling once more.

Lado came to Flower Hill with two huge trucks laden with his nine children, his fifth wife and his furniture. The

Flower Hill folk who came to watch whispered together, sized up Lado's wife like in-laws, then gave him a hand with the furniture. Under the envious gaze of the squatter women he took down from the trucks strange armchairs embroidered with silver threads and cupboards with mirrors. Their eyes were dazzled by embroidered cloths, tapestry cushions and shiny quilts. There were those who silently counted Lado's belongings one by one, and those who were envious of his wife. In the midst of the hut people's sighs Lado threw his things indoors and slept the sleep of the gambler. From then on the Flower Hill people began to witness Lado's true life-style. His wife grabbed the nine children they had brought and angrily threw them one by one into the street. 'Lado wants to sleep. You're a son of a bitch if you hang about', she said, chasing the squatters from the door. She threw stones at anyone still hanging about. She crouched in the street by her door with a long stick and a skirtful of stones. The hut people dispersed, laughing and chattering. Lado's wife never left the door until he woke up, and she kept the road quiet and clear of dogs, children, hens and squatters. When Lado got up and went tiptoeing to the coffeehouses in his gambling gear, his wife picked up the youngest child in her arms. Having left half the children behind to watch the house, and paired off the other half behind her, she set out to make herself better known to the squatters of Flower Hill. Strolling about amongst the huts she filled in the missing information about their lives. She described at length where they had lived before. She drew up accounts of the money Lado had lavished on her and told them proudly of his good qualities but she also wept and described how he beat her with a belt when she did not feel like sleeping with him. She cursed his previous wives one after the other and thumped the heads of the two children they had left behind as keepsakes. Led on by the crafty squatters to reveal her secrets, she forgot the time, while the women exchanged looks of amazement. She ignored the children who had dozed off around her and sat on into the small hours by the last door she had knocked at. Exhausted with gambling, Lado dragged his wife home and beat her until he made her yell. She wakened those who had struggled against her babble and who had finally managed to sleep. Nevertheless everyone on Flower Hill was delighted with all they had seen and heard in just one day.

Lado's arrival hurried on a phase in Flower Hill's history which would have happened even without him. This era was known by the title: 'Before the spring season when the coffeehouses opened'. It was full to overflowing with the songs, abuse and curses of the women whose husbands went off to the coffeehouse. The Flower Hill women turned against Lado, whose only fault was to enliven the days with the bright colours he wore, his peculiar adventures, and his affectations. As he walked along stretching his arms out, elbows bent, and wiggling his fingers (curled and stiff from holding cards), the women rushed from their homes into the streets. Some spat whole-heartedly after him.

A man who had lost a loan of ten thousand lira to Lado came home to his hut before dawn with a length of twine and tried to hang himself from the ceiling. His wife cut him down and, weeping, sang this song:

> *I knew he'd lost the game*
> *When he didn't meet my eye*

I knew Lado had won and was
Deep in sleep when the birds
Chose another way to fly.

The Flower Hill men stopped their ears against these mournful songs and, profiting from Lado's gambling skills and his inventive intelligence, developed all kinds of games and tricks designed to hoodwink their victims. The game which created the biggest impact — it made use of the ceilings being so low and so rotten — was the 'Early Morning Suicide Game'. It spread amongst the women as well as the men who sold their wives' gold jewellery for gambling, stole money from their wallets and sank heavily into debt. Three squatters who did not set up the game in quite the right way lost their lives at it. Street fights between men and women and raids on the coffeehouses by the children became daily events. The women waylaid Lado four times. They beat him up on three occasions and broke his chain with the devil's head. Both of his waistcoats were torn to shreds, and his wife and children could no longer step into the street.

As a result of all this the gamblers developed a code of their own, talks that had preceded the card games gradually turning into ceremonies of 'Respect for Gambling'. Every evening Lado put heart into them by recounting one of his adventures, and his listeners gave each other warm and lengthy handshakes. They attached iron bolts and nailed beams to the doors to prevent raids by the women, and a watch was set up to safeguard their gambling as it gradually bore fruit. Imitators of Lado appeared. It was deemed compulsory for every Flower Hill man to carry a pack of cards and dice instead of identification papers. Flower Hill differed from the other hut settlements in its zeal. It became a Gambler's Paradise.

Meantime the women kept up a continuous rain of stones at the coffeehouse windows and as they broke them one by one and as the owners put in new windows yet another coffeehouse was built. The new coffeehouses were tacitly shared amongst the gamblers. Those who could beat their wives into submission in the late hours left the coffeehouses and went back to their huts. Others who had broken loose from home spread mattresses on the chairs and their conversation, subdued and desultory, gradually died away as they fell asleep. Sitting smugly among his gambling companions, Lado reached for his winnings. In a tremulous voice he counted out his money but every night as he counted sweet sleep fled from his bed. Gazing into the darkness he tossed and turned as he yearned for sleep. All the same he would not let anyone else on the garbage hills challenge his status. Pursued by the curses of screeching women, he went his way in search of sleep with a gambler's trust in luck. And he was able to remain on Flower Hill until the son of Memet from the municipal police raided his gambling joint with a bread knife.

From the gamblers' coffeehouses a faint light was still shimmering on the howling dogs. Memet's wife who worked in the artificial detergent factory sat sighing and sleepless on the divan and, leaning her head against the window, she tearfully watched through the curtains a half moon and ten stars agleam in the sky. She pressed her roughened fingertips to her eyes and wept. Unable to bear his mother's weeping, Yıldırım grabbed the bread knife and rushed from the hut as though on horseback. By the time the sleepers had wakened to his mother's cries Yıldırım had reached the door of his father's favourite coffeehouse. Prodding the gamblers' watchman in the belly with the knife, he made him open the coffeehouse, then with his back to the door he showed his father the sharp blade he was holding. He trembled all over. 'Have you no shame?' he shouted and poured abuse on their obsession with gambling. He lectured them and declared that God would soon call them to account and that even tiny babies would pee on them. The gamblers sweated for shame, heads bent over the table, unable to look him in the face. Yıldırım felt sorry for them and began to speak gently in a way that touched their hearts. 'I am the same age as your own children,' he said. When he saw that some of the gamblers were weeping he went on at length, drawing energy from the knife he held. Memet got up and aimed a blow at his son who staggered and fell, then got back on his feet. Swearing viciously at his father Yıldırım returned the blow. When Lado tried to enter the fray Yıldırım stuck the knife in his belly then rushed out in fear, falling into the arms of the group of shouting women in front of the coffeehouse. Then he fainted, the babbling voices of the women exploding in his ears: 'Kill the lot, sweetheart, we'll look after you if you go to prison.'

Three women took Yıldırım away and pandemonium broke out in front of the coffeehouse. News took wing from Flower Hill that Lado had been knifed, and whoever was still asleep woke up. Lado, dripping blood, escaped by the back door, carried off by gamblers from another neighbourhood.

The morning after Lado ran away, there was a raid in the graveyard. Flower Hill, which had enjoyed its gambling joints and its fifteen coffeehouses as a result of the row over the Ramezan drum, once again displayed its ingenuity, managing to acquire a gang of marauders who stripped the huts of all their possessions, while the people were in hot pursuit of the meaning of 'anarchist'.

Repeated gunfire was heard from the graveyard, then it dwindled to a single shot and was silent. Three seagulls flying towards the silence heard that three young strangers hiding in the graveyard had come to Flower Hill to kill anyone who ventured out at night. The birds flew back screeching to the huts on the hill.

While the three young corpses were being removed from

Flower Hill, most of the squatters laughed at these 'bird-word' rumours. With the music of Lado's name still ringing in their ears, very few admitted to liking the foreign word 'anarchist'. Very few ever listened intently to the radio or cast an eye on a newspaper. Since the tough guys of the garbage hills had been trying to free the community for some time from the fear of being shot or killed, the passion for gambling outweighed the rumours. Fiery words soon died down after the graveyard episode but long before Flower Hill's name was inscribed on the map of the garbage hills, an underlying fear of the unfamiliar word 'anarchist' had begun to stir and spread among the folk. As the men sat in the coffeehouses, drugged with gambling, the word leapt out of the graveyard into the huts, feeding their fear, and soon those who had lost their mates and had to walk by themselves hardly dared go near the graveyard. After the workers' quarters were searched, the Flower Hill women seized on this foreign word, and those who wanted to frighten their husbands told a string of horror stories which spread to the huts. Certain prominent squatters, whose profound and special knowledge had impressed the community, vied with one another to settle the meaning of 'anarchist', and competition fanned the flames of fear. Ill-omened comments on Yıldırım's speech to the gamblers and his stabbing of Lado began to get around and he ran away from Flower Hill, afraid of being mistaken for an anarchist. His flight gave people the idea that anarchists must be sheltering in their midst. One of the squatters tried to talk himself out of his fear by introducing the unsuitable subject of a man called 'Bolshie Memet' who had killed 99 people in his village.

That very night four daredevil youths of Flower Hill one by one wrapped themselves up and wound black yashmaks round their heads, and from then on not a single squatter could be seen in the back streets at night. Flower Hill groaned under the oppression of the 'Black Gang' which did not actually murder people venturing out at night but did succeed in gradually undermining their lives. Within a month there was no-one left on Flower Hill who had not lost half his earnings to the 'Black Gang'. The number who emptied their pockets into the Black Gang's hands in just three nights running topped 1500. On the fourth night Sefer the janitor broke down in tears and sobs, and beat his children for not crying along with him.

The hut people's common sense — and no-one had yet discovered where it lurked in a human being — could find no good reason why a bank should open a branch on Flower Hill at that time. A crowd of squatters gathered in curiosity at the door of the bank and their children shouted and snatched flowers off the garlands hanging against the walls. Those flowers too, like others on Flower Hill, afflicted by pollution from the factories, wilted before anyone could smell them. But when the bank opened Flower Hill acquired one more avenue and a gleaming blue 'Bank Avenue' was hung over the street.

On the opening day Garbage Chief swaggered in with his money and created a commotion, boasting of the benefits to be gained. This forged a bond between the bank and the community. The daughter of a squatter, famous on Flower Hill for his stubbornness, brought two chickens to put in Garbage Chief's fridge: 'Tell your father to put money in the bank instead of eating chickens', Garbage Chief carelessly suggested. The girl put in the chickens and rushed back to tell her father what Garbage Chief had said. Her father whose tough argumentative temperament had earned him the name 'Colonel' rushed out of his hut and made straight for Garbage Chief's door. He angrily demanded his two chickens back and returned home. The very next day he bought a refrigerator, set it against the wall of his hut and, when he had consoled himself somewhat for the insult, went to the bank and put in all his money.

News of this event spread through Flower Hill and increased the Colonel's reputation. But when he took out his savings book and showed it off to anyone he could collar, a certain chill entered into his relations with the squatters. 'Anyone can put anything they like in my refrigerator,' he bragged, and his wife irritated the Flower Hill people and got on the women's nerves with her 'All our money is in the bank, thanks to Garbage Chief.' Everyone went and bought a refrigerator where Garbage Chief had bought his and took it to their hut and, setting it against the wall, went off to the bank in ones and twos. Their hearts overflowed with joy as they thrust their savings books into their bosoms, but an endless race for possessions followed. Whenever anyone bought anything for their hut the rest only had to see it to follow suit. Soon the tradesmen discovered the inclinations of the Flower Hill people. One of them managed to sell a set of liqueur glasses to every woman on Flower Hill and from another tradesman all the squatter women bought red net curtains.

While the race for possessions on Flower Hill was going full speed ahead, Kurd Cemal built a cinema in the middle of the garbage hills, the cinema the squatters had all dreamed of long ago. A squatter who stayed at home hungry because of his humpback and was insultingly known as 'Lentil' beause of his stature, found a way to fill his belly by hefting a sandwich board about — a new experience for Flower Hill. He tossed it up on his hump and began to shout the patter he had learned by heart,'Love, cruelty, bloodshed, bitter revenge'. His convincing voice boomed through the settlement and turned the race for possessions into a race for the cinema.

In the cinema Crazy Gönül dropped asleep.

At the cinema door her face was wet with rain. When the man in the ticket-office saw the water dripping from Crazy Gönül's hair and lashes, he let her in without payment. Crazy Gönül skipped in gleefully. 'Have you no home, girl?' asked the ticket man. Crazy Gönül shrugged and stuck out her tongue at him. The ticket man grabbed at her breast but Crazy Gönül jumped back swearing and he laughed.

Crazy Gönül's husband — Huge apartment blocks

He walked wearily along the street of apartment blocks, a carpet on his shoulder. In the next street he stopped and looked up, and his glance collided with the scream of a loudly-painted goldenhaired woman. Then two porters appeared alongside Crazy Gönül's astonished husband. While selling the carpet he was arrested for stealing it and thrown into prison where he ripped open a man's belly.

Crazy Gönül — Huts of trumpets and whistles

Flower Hill of fading light and nearby factory chimneys. Twilight. Crazy Gönül's eyes searched the streets for her husband. But they led her to where she found a woman who had a job as manual worker in the Flower Hill Industries and whose husband was now in prison. She begged her to take her along too when she went to visit her husband. Crazy Gönül yelled and screamed and stamped on the prison floor with rage, then returned to her hut where she slept all alone. A craftsman with dark eyebrows, a cutter in one of the textile workshops of the Flower Hill Industries, took an interest in Crazy Gönül's loneliness. 'Let's make you something nice to wear', he suggested with a leer. Crazy Gönül's eyes darted gleefully here and there and settled on some flowery material which the black-browed craftsman held against her, caressing her shoulders. He smelled her hair and played with it. From the flowery material he made her a dress with a gathered skirt and a wide neck, and when she put it on it turned her head. She sat on the lap of the craftsman with the black eyebrows but his knees ached as she struggled and kicked, so he pushed her off to a fellow craftsman. Crazy Gönül went from knee to knee and finally left Flower Hill for far away. And for two years she was not seen on the garbage hills.

Two years later she returned to Flower Hill accompanied by an old man and she bore her aged friend from hut to hut like a workbag, introducing him as 'Amem Şemsi's husband'. Before long a flock of Amem Şemsi's relations, friends and acquaintances swarmed over the place and as the number of people asking for Crazy Gönül's hut increased, the squatters left off calling behind them 'Are you a teacher?' The hut people thought that the well-dressed strangers lost in the streets must be teachers, but when they realized the true state of affairs they made their disapproval very clear. Crazy Gönül began to get angry at their sour looks. 'If you think you're any better than me you can fill my belly!' she said. The Flower Hill men pulled knives on three clients who came knocking on her door and when she opened up she was given the official title of 'The First Whore of Flower Hill'. 'I've got to live!' she said as she took in the strangers amidst shouting and fighting. Amem Şemsi's husband could not bear the fights any longer and stopped dragging along beside Crazy Gönül. He gave up the ghost and died. And when Crazy Gönül's support had passed on, then Flower Hill acknowledged her as their first whore who could be bought for a bagful of grapes and a lump of cheese. Some of the men kept a credit account with her, and she got into fights with those who did not pay. She attacked their wives and stoned the squatters' windows, weeping with rage. Her eyes clouded with fury, and it was only at the cinema that they shone like glass. When her distress became too great she thrust her bare feet into her nylon slippers and ran to the cinema.

> *Slipper bird, slipper bird*
> *Flap flap slipper bird*

Flower Hill's appetite swelled high to the skies above the garbage hills as this slipper bird flew amongst the huts. Every day that passed the number of women racing to the cinema increased. They shed many a tear on the roads until they discovered that the film stars had not really died, but once the tears were dried the young girls started to go about with bare arms and legs like film stars and the women cast off their headscarves. Fired with the desire for pleasure after Tirintaz Fidan's night lessons, women now clung to their husbands' hands and feet begging for love. They trembled and swooned with upturned eyes and uttered strangled sobs at not being loved, but their men who were gambling their lives away in the coffeehouses brought them back down to earth with a beating.

Hacı Hasan, the muezzin in one of the mosques of the tin minarets, was shocked by the Flower Hill women's immodest dress and while he strolled quietly in the mosque courtyard, thinking, 'Lord, what will become of these women!' his own daughter, famous on Flower Hill for having read the Koran twenty-seven times from cover to cover, was stricken with an incurable illness. She was unable to appear in public or even at her window. No matter how many prayers Hacı Hasan recited over his daughter, she did not recover and the malady carried her off to the next world. The squatters duly wept together and took her up and buried her in the graveyard. Before a month was out the girl had risen from the grave and returned to her father's hut, weeping bitterly and with arms and legs severely burned. 'It's God's punishment!' said the muezzin and sat his daughter down on the divan, her head covered by a fine white muslin with hand-embroidered edges. He put up a cotton curtain to separate the divan from the room, and he hid his daughter behind the curtain. He went round every single mosque on Flower Hill, whispering to the imams that his daughter had risen and come back from the other world. Even before he got home Flower Hill was on its feet; it was not clear who had spread the news.

Behind her curtain the muezzin's daughter softly read a verse from the Koran to the people crowding the hut. Then she revealed that God had brought her back to this world as a lesson to the women who walked with bare legs and arms and their hair uncovered. She hid her face in white muslin and showed her burned arms through the folds of the curtain to the women huddled together in fear.

When the news reached other areas of the garbage hills, the ground before the muezzin's hut became like the place of gathering on the Day of Judgement. At midnight the squatters waiting their turn to speak to the muezzin's daughter were sent away at her request, buzzing in alarm and hanging on to each other's skirts and arms. When the crowd had withdrawn, the muezzin peeled off the beeswax blackened with soot which had covered her arms and legs, and the exhausted girl collapsed on the divan and fell asleep. In the morning the muezzin called his daughter at the hour of prayer, smeared her legs and arms again with beeswax and renewed the soot. After he had blackened her limbs he prepared his hut for visitors. The girl rehearsed under her breath new warnings learned from her father and sat down on the divan. And before a single morsel could pass her lips people were leaving their huts and gathering at her door.

Some time later inhabitants of the city's other shanty-towns began to stream to Flower Hill. The muezzin's hut became a convalescent home where people came and went in search of a remedy for their troubles. Hacı the Muezzin began to pray and breathe over barren women and to produce charms and amulets for broken hearts. Although he would accept no money from those who spoke with his daughter, he did not refuse sugar, tea and rice. When there was no more room in his hut he came to an agreement with a grocer for the sackfuls of sugar, tea and rice. One day a week he closed his hut to visitors and went off to sell. Within three days his sacks were filled again to the brim by squatter women who had covered up their legs and arms or wrapped themselves in black cloaks and were asking for news from the other world. And while the sacks were filling up the muezzin's daughter waxed lyrical. She described the trees, the water melons and sweet melons, the houses and rivers of the other world. She imitated the screams of people plunged from boiling water into icy cold for going to the cinema in this world and forsaking prayer and fasting. Behind the curtain she uttered little moans. The hoarse strangled sound was overheard by the police and one afternoon they raided the hut. The muezzin was tied up and sent to prison. The girl stripped the beeswax from her arms and legs and ran off to find a husband.

The Flower Hill women underwent a crisis of belief after this, and their faces showed traces of deep confusion. They plastered make-up on their cheeks and lips and around their eyes to hide the traces and when they reappeared, beaten black and blue as never before, the multi-coloured clouds of the Flower Hill Industries burst open from envy.

Şini Erol, the president of Flower Hill Sports Club, raced about the huts whipping up the young workmen in the repair shops to dream of becoming football stars. The shining hero of the Flower Hill football team was Hıdır who pursued this dream so fervently that he beat up his mother day and night for money so that he could eat his daily ration of half a kilo of hazel nuts which Şini Erol had recommended instead of milk and eggs. Hıdır's brothers in the dream chose the same method of extracting money and one by one the women of Flower Hill were subjected to the 'Hazelnut Ordeal'.

Şini Erol sold glass, mirrors and birds in Factory Foot Quarter and devoted his life to the young gypsies and squatters for the love of football. Before a match he shut up the flower of the team in his shop, got to work on their backs and gave them all a thorough massage. The match over, he gathered the team and took them to the hamam where he carefully kneaded their backs, fronts and legs. The hamam outing was followed by orders of new bread for everybody, hot from the oven and spread with two packets of margarine for each player, all part of the diet. Every time they scored Şini Erol kissed the lobes of their ears and when one of the young men fell out with his father, Erol put up a bed in his shop and stayed the night with him.

While Şini Erol, in the words of the hut people, was 'playing a hot game' in the shop, Flower Hill resounded with news that was to ruin the happiness of all the huts including Şini Erol's shop. They heard that in thirty days the government would tear down the homes built on the garbage hills. Garbage Chief with the Elders of Flower Hill behind him set off for the municipal office. But before they had even got down to Panty Way, the hut people had set up another committee of three, charged with the job of finding a piece of land suitable for hut building in the hills behind the city. The committee explored the far reaches of the city for three days and found a flat hilltop which overlooked the dazzling blue sea from among the pines. In alarm Garbage Chief made moves to prevent his leadership slipping from his grasp, but finally joined the Committee for Hut Locations. He abandoned his hut after being reassured that he would be made headman again, and off he went to the flat hill.

When the government heard that the Flower Hill folk were digging up and dividing the top of a hill overlooking the dazzling blue sea, they gave up the idea of destroying Flower Hill. They produced a document informing Flower Hill that the area on which it stood was the property of something called a Foundation and called upon the people to pay a settlement fee of 70,000 lira each. They announced that those who paid this sum could live in the huts, provided they all paid a yearly rent to the Foundation. After the announcement, the first step was to split up families, and brides, the elderly and children were charged with keeping watch on the flat hilltop which overlooked the dazzling blue sea. The others became responsible for the future of Flower Hill.

Mustafa Gülibik had a job in a workshop at the Flower Hill Industries producing armchair tassels. Spurred on by the squatters, he made a stirring speech before the municipal office which began, 'Ataturk, for whom I would willingly lay down my life . . . ' He told how his grandfather had gone to fight in the First World War; even the hunting dog had followed him and wasn't seen for seven years but returned with him from the war. He described how the dog, faithful to its owner, had made the whole village weep and did not forget to mention that his grandfather and his dog died fighting the Greeks. 'Ataturk gave Flower Hill into our keeping', he spluttered, flinging the words at the municipal office. As he tried to gather strength his face became bathed in sweat. Wiping away the sweat with one hand, he raised the other in the air and swore an oath that they would never hand over Flower Hill to be anyone else's property. Elated by the squatters' excited shouts and yells, he lost his head and let slip that he would do God knows what obscene act to the Foundation. The Flower Hill people applauded him warmly for this. He finished up speaking nervously in spurts and broken words and poured out curse after curse. The police who were trying to disperse the people had to fire in the air.

Cursing and swearing, the squatters made their way back to Flower Hill, and an argument erupted as to whether Mustafa Gülibik had spoken inappropriately.

Some of the hut people agreed that although they had applauded him, there was no place for bad language in a speech, and others claimed that Flower Hill had nothing at all to do with wars past and gone. It emerged from these arguments, which ended in a beating for Mustafa Gülibik, that not only his grandfather's dog but the dogs of all the grandfathers of the Flower Hill folk had gone to the war. But while the squatters were gathered together in their houses telling competing dog stories, four smartly dressed men who said they had come to Flower Hill from the Foundation looked round the huts. They collected money and gave false receipts and they left behind four more dog stories.

Nothing more was heard from the smartly dressed men and the suspicion grew that their stories had not been true either. The squatters who worked as regular municipal garbage collectors were asked to investigate. Much later the garbage collectors brought news that Flower Hill's name had been erased from the map of the garbage hills and FOUNDATION had been written in red in its place. At the news, the word 'Foundation' suddenly took fire on the squatters' tongues. They amicably drew up petitions together, signed them and went in a body to the police station and the municipal office. No one ever discovered what this 'Foundation' really was: what finally emerged was simply a new name for Flower Hill.

The Flower Hill people had set out as a community to found new quarters by dividing up the flat hilltop, and had already given it the name 'Unity Neighbourhood'. But when they discovered that the name of Flower Hill had been struck off the map, they decided to call their new quarters 'Unity Flower Hill' instead.

Unity Flower Hill was so far, so very far away from

*Foundation Hill that Flower Hill children who set off
from there could only see the sky.*

The Flower Hill people's attempts to inhabit these two neighbourhoods simultaneously exhausted the children. The dream of the old and infirm was to see Unity Hill with their mortal eyes before they went on their pilgrimage to Mecca. As people shuttled to and fro between Flower Hill and Unity Hill, it became customary to see them off with tears and welcome them back with embraces. Every day the hut people took a few of their belongings to Unity Hill and after their final crowning move, the name Unity Hill survived for ever. But the new name, Foundation Hill, fell from favour and did not last a year. Several different names like 'Flower Hill — Hashish Hiding Hole' or 'Flower Hill — Nest of Whores' took its place.

While the Flower Hill people were going crazy between the two communities great numbers of men were fired from the Rubbish Road factories with their silent workers and noisy machines, and the Flower Hill women heard they would be taken on instead of the men. The Flower Hill girls gathered round factory doors were asked if they intended to get engaged, and the women if they intended to have babies. Those who were not going to marry or have a child were taken on and put to work. The result was broken engagements and a rush to the midwife to get rid of babies swelling in their wombs. When the women came to work on Rubbish Road, Unity Hill was left to the old and the men. With most women working on Flower Hill and their men on Unity Hill a condition called 'the family disaster' reared its head.

Three Flower Hill men had postponed marrying a second wife from Unity Hill because of an alert that the huts there might be demolished, but as soon as the danger was over they each looked around and took a second wife. Then one of the legally married wives murdered her fellow-wife with two stabs of the knife in the street. Another legal wife came from Foundation Hill to Unity Hill to stir up trouble and was carved up by her husband who had taken a second wife. After that, the third squatter's new wife took all her bits and pieces and ran away. This woman managed to save her life, but the number of men and women who failed to save their lives increased every day. Ehmail the squatter who ran the grocery shop on Unity Hill heard that his wife who worked on Foundation Hill in the bulb factory had gone bareheaded and tossed her hair in the men's faces as she passed the coffeehouses. He set out for Foundation Hill and tore out her hair until she bled. Some time later, when they had gone for a stroll one evening and she had refused his arm, he played the dictator even further. Forcing his wife back into his hut he strangled her with a piece of wire.

Although the other male squatters did not turn out as tyrannical as Ehmail, those women who lived on Foundation Hill and managed not to get shot or stabbed were considered to be of 'exceptional ingenuity'. But Unity Hill became the stage for their raids, and only two male squatters succeeded in raising a family there with their second wives.

The coffeehouses, empty now since the men's withdrawal from Foundation Hill, were taken over by male squatters from other neighbourhoods and by workers and their bosses from the Rubbish Road repair sheds, and when the gypsies moved downhill a little from their cardboard houses, this put the finishing touch to Foundation Hill. The upper floors of the workshops in the Flower Hill Industries filled up with 'Knocking Shops' crowded with bareheaded, barelegged women whom the squatters called 'Them'. 'They' kept their shops closed by day but at night they started up playing and singing and the huts vibrated with piercing whistles.

From the first day she set foot on Foundation Hill everyone's attention was drawn to a huge woman, one of 'Them'. This woman, whose name was Emel, had muscular legs like a man's, a huge head and cropped hair dyed yellow. Whereas many of 'Them' with provocative names like Angèle and Marie walked with downcast eyes, Emel brazenly paced the streets like a loaded mule, indifferent to the squatters who cursed her to her face. One step in every three she stopped and raised her jutting chin, then took one step forward wagging her butt three times to right and left and swinging her breasts. Soon after Emel came to Foundation Hill the squatter women in their homes were giggling and mimicking her walk. She grew famous amongst them as 'Emel the Mule', but in the coffeehouses she was known as the 'Half-Hour Lay' — from her boast to men that no man ever lay with her for less than half an hour. Those who heard the sad story of her life from her own lips broke down in tears and everyone knew how her husband had gone to prison for robbery and had killed a man there. All the garbage hill neighbourhoods heard of her accomplished swearing at men who whistled after her but it was rumoured that the 'Half-Hour Lay' was a fake. There were heated arguments amongst the men as to whether or not she was a genuine woman. She swore at the men who wanted 'a half-hour lay', and tried showing her breasts. But the pleasure she took in her walk was spoiled by these rumours. The testimony of a squatter postman who had seen her in a distant neighbourhood sitting amongst women with a baby in her arms, was not considered valid. Every time the 'Half-Hour Lay' passed the coffeehouses she was insulted and attacked. Finally rejecting Foundation Hill where people at every corner touched her up and cheered her on to bare her breasts, she departed swearing and crying.

When Emel the Mule had gone, Crazy Gönül's star rose again. She often reminded them of Emel's walk and her way of swearing and laughing. There was a sudden increase in the number of men rapping at her door, and the young men of Foundation Hill, with their predilection for the 'Knocking Shop' names, called her 'Kristin'.

While Kristin ran about among the huts weeping and swearing, 'Night Clubs' opened up in the narrow alleys off the main road. Yellow, blue and red lightbulbs — the kind that flashed on and off — were fixed to the doors of the night clubs, but the lights winking at the huts died out within three days. The gypsies waiting to perform at the night clubs played the most lively airs on such touching strings that the melancholy of people who had come to shed their depression melted away in drifting clouds of smoke. Seductive coquettes seated side by side some way from the tables leaned forward to reveal their bosoms and licked their pouting lips with pink tongues, but failed to console the clients. People slipping into a melancholy coma under the influence of alcohol and gypsy music were secretly offered hashish. They flew with the drug and, with fluttering wings, alighted on the gypsy tree of life. And for those who alighted, the gypsies opened the door to worlds of feeling and perception. Intimacies which began in the night clubs grew stronger in the cardboard neighbourhood and in the coffeehouses of Foundation Hill. After some time the gypsy way of life overshadowed the squatters who lived on Foundation Hill. Fragments of the gypsy language passed into the squatters' slang and gypsy rhymes like 'Aynur gudunur, Ayudum gudumu' entered the children's games. Gypsy children carried bags of lotto counters and hung about every corner on Flower Hill. In the early hours of the morning the gypsy women left the cardboard neighbour-hood, bosoms stuffed with cigarette packets, and scattered through the streets of Knocking Shops. And now Güllü Baba's last dream, forgotten by the squatters, came true.

People overflowed onto Foundation Hill to see the community of huts founded on the crust of the garbage hills, the gleaming garbage slopes and the grass and flowers sprouting from the iridescence. Until the workers from the Rubbish Road factories appeared on the scene waving their banners, the gypsy voices went on echoing round Flower Hill.

Flower Hill   *Gudu Hill*

Acknowledgements

The translators wish to thank John Berger for his belief in the book and for his consistent interest, good will and encouragement.

Thanks are due to Michael Freeman for his numerous helpful suggestions and for his enthusiasm and sympathetic support throughout the project.

Above all we owe a tremendous debt of gratitude to Latife Tekin who has never failed to respond generously to requests for occasional clarification and background information.